THE
EARTH
SINGS

YA DING

THE
EARTH
SINGS

Translated by
JON ROTHSCHILD

A Helen and Kurt Wolff Book

Harcourt Brace Jovanovich, Publishers

SAN DIEGO   NEW YORK   LONDON

First published in French as *Le Sorgho rouge*.

Library of Congress Cataloging-in-Publication Data
Ding, Ya.
[Sorgho rouge. English]
The Earth Sings/Ya Ding; translated by Jon Rothschild.—1st ed.
p.   cm.
Translation of: Le sorgho rouge.
"A Helen and Kurt Wolff book."
ISBN 0-15-176140-X
I. Title.
PQ3979.2.D56S6713   1989
843—dc20   89-15646

Design by Camilla Filancia
Printed in the United States of America

First edition   A B C D E

To my father

and to my dear friends

JoËLLE NEUDIN

and

CHRISTIAN THIMONIER

PART ONE

Liang put his hand over his mouth to keep from choking on the yellow dust. Thrown up by the wheels of the cart and the plodding donkey, it fell over them like a veil, shutting them in. Near him, his little sister moaned.

They were changing countries, traveling through a dusty screen of shadow and sun. The scrawny, hairless donkey had been pulling the cart since last night, and the constant creaking had been plowing furrows in Liang's brain. He counted: five steps, two jolts, five steps, two jolts, five steps . . . The bumps in the road and the creaking seemed endless. Where, where are we going? Maybe the old donkey, pulling them along through whirlwinds of dust, knew. After all, he had white tufts of hair in his ears—just like old Gao, his father's friend in their town who was a Party leader and had been on the Long March with Chairman Mao, so he had to be very old. The donkey could not ask questions, but Liang could. He had the right, though he was only nine and a half years old. They had wanted him to come, so they must need him. "Is everyone here?" his father had asked. Which meant that if Liang had not been there, his sister alone would not have been enough to make them a family. But Liang was not the one who decided things. He belonged to the family like an object, like the red wooden trunk his father had hoisted into the back of the cart. That's the way things were: parents decided; children obeyed.

They were changing countries. Shadow. Sun.

Yesterday they had been in their town. Today they were in some other place. Was it possible that no one knew where? His father could have told them something, made some comment, the way he did when the table was dirty or when he wound his watch. Just the other day, for instance, he had put his hand on Liang's shoulder after dinner and said, "We're going to the movies tonight." A few words that didn't cost him much: he had been picking his teeth when he said them. But it had made Liang happy. Someone had said something, no matter how careless the tone. It was good to know what was going to happen. Liang had walked with more confidence that night. A good idea, going to the movies, he had said to himself, as though he had decided it. Unfortunately, it usually wasn't that way. Most of the time, grownups took you wherever they wanted, without a word of explanation, just as they were doing now. And there was no fun in thinking about what was coming next. Just boredom and worry.

Where are we going?

Five steps, two jolts . . . No way to ask, no way to open your mouth, not on this road, with its bumps, yellow dust, and pebbles digging into your ribs and stinging your sides. Open your mouth, and dust would fly in. And the sun, beating down, was a thousand glittering needles that forced you to close your eyes.

The chittering of cicadas sounded almost like a war cry. Were they angered by these strangers in their midst? Maybe they would attack the donkey, the cart, the family. Liang opened his eyes a crack despite the sun, trying to see where the cicadas were. He saw nothing.

It would be better if he let himself slip into a kind of stupor. No point in worrying. All he had to do was sleep

4

until the cart stopped; then he would find out where they were.

"Mama, I'm thirsty," Ling complained, trying to pull off the white scarf her mother had knotted over her head to protect her from the sun.

Wang handed her the old black pitcher. Ling grabbed it, pressed her mouth to the clay spout, and drank greedily, making a noise that sounded like a stream gurgling over pebbles.

Their father, motionless, his back rigid, seemed to ignore the jostling of the cart. In his left hand he held the reins, in his right a willow branch with which he flicked the donkey's hairless rump absent-mindedly. Was he staring at something in the distance, something that lay at the end of this bumpy road?

Liang got thirsty watching his sister drink. "I want some too," he could have said to his mother. But he didn't want to hear the inevitable "After your sister." It was embarrassing. It had been that way ever since this little sister had come into the world: whenever he wanted something, she asked for the same thing, and usually got it first.

"Don't you want some, Liang?" she asked, but she put her mouth to the spout again. He knew she wasn't really drinking, because he couldn't hear that annoying gurgle. She was just playing with the spout, making a whistling sound.

"Are you asleep, Liang?" his mother asked.

Liang did not answer, taking a perverse pleasure in his silence. Pretending to be asleep was a smart thing to do. You could watch what others were doing, and they wouldn't know it. No one thought about you when you were asleep, or at least they didn't think about what you were thinking. It was as though you weren't there.

"Are you asleep, Liang?" his mother asked again.

"Let him sleep," said Li, flicking the donkey's rump more sharply.

The donkey balked. The cart veered into the field beside the road, crushing three cornstalks. Everyone yelled or swore except Liang, who was still pretending to be asleep.

Li jumped out of the cart. He pulled the idiotic donkey as hard as he could, trying to turn it back toward the road, but the donkey refused to budge. There was more strength in that hairless neck than in Liang's father's hands. His father pulled. The donkey braced itself. A draw. Liang, his eyes half-open, felt good lying there in the cart, his head on a sack of jute, watching the battle. He was sure his father would win in the end. How could a donkey win against a Party functionary? Liang shook his head to drive out such a ridiculous thought.

Dust rose in eddies around the cart and drifted down on the combatants, whose bodies glistened with sweat. The sun's rays seemed like bursts of laughter.

The cart leaned forward, and Li gave up. Exhausted, he let go of the donkey, and the donkey stopped pulling. "What now?" Li mumbled, scratching at the mud that had formed on his face from the mixture of sweat and dust.

"Maybe it's thirsty," Ling shouted, holding the old pitcher out toward the donkey.

"It must be tired," Wang said, pushing the pitcher back. "How far have we come since morning?"

"About four miles, I guess," Liang's father said.

"Is it much farther?"

"We're halfway, more or less."

It was ridiculous: Liang couldn't keep pretending to be asleep. He had to say what he thought, help his father get the stupid donkey out of the field, make it get those stiff legs moving again. His own leg hurt too: the big wooden trunk had hit him once when the cart swerved. That donkey! He felt like kicking it.

Should he wave his arms and yell "Mama!" or just get up quietly? Which would be more natural? He never should have pretended to be asleep.

The donkey, now calm, was trying to eat the cornstalks through its muzzle. Wang got out of the cart and picked Ling up.

"He's strange, that boy," said Li, looking at Liang.

"Well, he was not happy to leave our town."

"I am," the little girl said.

Li took off the donkey's muzzle and fed it the crushed cornstalks.

"Too bad there are no trees." Wang sighed. "We could have rested in a shady spot."

"You!" The voice startled them. "You shouldn't let your donkey graze in a cornfield!" A peasant pushing a wheelbarrow full of corn came up behind them.

"You're right. But I can't make the bastard do what it's told," Li said.

The peasant looked at them with suspicion. "Don't you know a donkey always does the opposite of what you tell it? If you want to get it out of the field, try to push it farther in. Otherwise, you'll be here all day."

Putting down his wheelbarrow, he walked over to the donkey. He wore faded rags, and his sunburned face, his eyes buried under thick eyebrows, made it impossible to guess his age. He seized the donkey by the neck and pushed him toward the field. The donkey leaned the opposite way, answering each shove by a step toward the man. After three or four shoves, the donkey was back on the road.

"You've done it, Uncle!" said Wang.

"Thank you so much, Grandfather," added Ling.

"What a good little girl." The peasant chuckled, happy with what he'd done. "Where are you going?" he asked.

"Xin Zhuang," Li answered.

"That's where I'm from . . ." The man blinked. "You wouldn't be Prefect Li, would you?"

"Why, yes," said Li, astonished. "How did you know?"

"I don't know anything," the peasant muttered, suddenly changing his tone and looking worried. He grabbed his wheelbarrow.

"Is it far from here, Uncle?" Wang asked.

"About seven miles," the peasant called over his shoulder.

"Peculiar," Li murmured, watching him walk away. Then the family set out again.

The sun, motionless in the sky ahead, covered the dull landscape with an incandescent shroud, a white flame. Dust swirled and rose around them. The donkey's hoofs made the only sound. There were no ponds or streams, none of the fields Liang saw in his dreams, just dried, cracked mud. The family went deeper and deeper into a wretched landscape of tired corn and shriveled sorghum.

Liang curled up like the leaves, closing his eyes, his mouth, his hands, even his feet. He thought of school; of his friends; of the desk on which, with his penknife and much care, he had carved the names of heroes of great battles; of the bench he had so often measured in a useless effort to divide it equally with the little girl he shared it with. All these everyday things, which once bored him, now seemed special. School would start again tomorrow, but he wouldn't be there. He hadn't even said good-bye. All the pranks he had dreamed up with his friends were wasted now. No; it was worse than that. He was what was wasted. He had left his friends, possibly for good, and they didn't even know where he was. Neither did he. He didn't know where he was or where he was going.

Xin Zhuang, his father had said. Xin Zhuang. What did it mean? Maybe Xin Zhuang was a village. But where?

You're supposed to be asleep, Liang, he reminded himself. You almost forgot. If you want to ask questions, you have to wake up first. Lord of Heaven, what a bad idea faking sleep had been.

The cart climbed a slope. On the way down, the donkey broke into a trot, making the cart rattle and bounce. Li pulled back on the reins as hard as he could, but the donkey, its neck arched like a harp, continued to trot. Li hit angrily with the branch, and the donkey broke into a gallop. Liang's head hit hard wood. He hurt all over. He tried to turn on his side, moaning the way he did in the morning when his mother came to shake him awake: "Come, Liang, time to get up."

Then suddenly the donkey decided to drop into a walk again. Liang put his head back on the jute pillow. Having slept through all those violent bumps, he had no choice now but to stay asleep. Luckily, no one was paying any attention to him.

Peering between the planks of the side of the cart, Liang watched the countryside go by. He heard dogs barking. They had come to a village. It was a little place of wooden huts with slanted thatched roofs; they faced south, the direction of the winds on this plain. The paper windows, yellowed by sun and rain, looked like wide, menacing eyes designed to scare away intruders.

Three small boys, thin and naked, holding hands, came out of an alley between two huts. They stopped in the sunlight. When Liang's family looked at them, the boys ran back into the shadow between the huts. An old woman in rags came out, balancing a child on her right hip and holding a chipped clay washbowl in her left hand. She looked at them and dropped the bowl. A hen standing on a mound of dung stuck its head under some straw, showing its red and featherless rump.

The cart rolled away from the village. Li turned in his seat, unable to take his eyes off the wretched huts, which seemed to sink into the ground, holding on to one another to slow their fall.

"What a miserable place!" Wang exclaimed.

"The place has to be poor, or there's no point in it," Li said, as though talking to himself.

"Poor . . . no point in it." What did that mean? No point in what? Liang did not understand. Would they have to live in a village like that? Would skinny children be his friends? They looked like skeletons or ghosts. Why did they run and hide like that? What did they do all day? "Miserable," his mother had said.

Too many questions spun around in Liang's head, like the wheels of the cart as it passed one sorghum field after another.

Liang fell asleep.

"Wake up, Liang! We're here." It was Ling's shrill voice.

Liang sat up. He rubbed his eyes, stretched, and yawned, opening his mouth wide. He saw a huge gray sky. For a moment, he thought he was in the town, but there was a silence deep inside him he'd never felt before, an emptiness, as though something had left for good. Then he remembered: the donkey's plodding, the sound of the cicadas, the creaking of the axles, the make-believe sleep. Town was far away. It had left him like a ship that slipped its moorings.

"Did you sleep well?" Li asked with a smile.

"Now you won't be able to get to sleep tonight," Wang said anxiously.

Liang did not answer.

He looked around him. The land was just as endless as before, but its earlier brightness under the whitish-yellow sun had dissolved into gray. The sky, too, had lost its light. Dull clouds hung over the desolate surrounding fields, reaching down to them. Great sheets of salt, crusty white, gave pearly glimmers here and there. It was an upside-down world, in which the ground had swallowed the sky, and the sky was only the ground's reflection. Scrawny stalks of sorghum poked up through the dust in places. In the distance was the silhouette of a village; from it, an arrow pierced the deepening twilight.

"What's that?" Liang asked, staring at it.

"It's a steeple," his father said.

"What's a steeple?"

"A steeple is a tower with a bell inside," his mother said in her schoolteacher voice. "Under the bell there's usually a church."

Church? Liang remembered the word from a book they had read in school. It had something to do with God, religion, ghosts, and the Great Lord of Heaven—things that didn't have much to do with people. He looked at the steeple. Grayer than the twilight and high in the clouds, it seemed to be trying to push back the sky.

"That's a ten," his little sister said, pointing to the cross at the top of the tower.

They saw it more clearly when they got closer. At the very top of the steeple, the large wooden cross floating in the sea of clouds looked just like the character for the numeral ten.

The cart, axles creaking, began to climb the slope leading into the village. Li got down and led the donkey by its bridle.

Darkness was separating them from this strange new world. Liang felt as though their steps were bound by chains, like the prisoners he had once seen in town, who were not allowed to take a single step off the path. What invisible guards were watching over them now, leading them into the unknown, into what he felt would be a kind of prison?

He thought he heard something: a sound from far off, three high notes repeated twice. It sounded magical; it seemed to change the feel of the air and the color of the night.

He turned around, but saw nothing. He looked everywhere; still nothing. Then he thought that the sound might be inside his own ears, which had been pressed too hard against the jute pillow. The others didn't seem to hear anything. It was the cart's creaking that filled the thickening night.

When they reached the top of the slope, the donkey stopped.

"Mama, that smells good!" Ling said.

"Yes. It's suppertime in the village."

Liang saw some boys and girls about his age sitting on the doorstep of the first house. Each had a bowl, and they were eating happily, but they stopped to watch the cart roll by.

A big yellow dog came up behind the cart and growled. A little girl dressed in red offered it a piece of black bread. With a stifled whine, the dog snatched it, and the little girl smiled shyly at Liang.

Two white banners hung on a large arched gate. One said, in red characters, COMMUNE COMMITTEE OF THE CHINESE COMMUNIST PARTY; the other, in black characters, said COMMITTEE OF THE XIN ZHUANG PEOPLE'S COMMUNE.

A group of men, who had been waiting at the gate, came toward them. The leader was a tall, stout man, older than his father, with a black beard that covered his face up to his shining eyes. His sleeveless peasant jacket and baggy trousers, held at the waist by a cord, were made of unbleached linen.

"You must be tired, Prefect Li," he said loudly, grasping Li's hand as though he were a long-lost brother and smiling as if this was the happiest day of his life. "I am Zhao Jialu."

The powerful voice startled Liang.

"I am sorry to have kept you waiting," Li said, shaking the man's hand.

"May I present Comrade Song, who is also a member

of the Committee. She is in charge of the women of the commune."

Song reached out timidly to shake hands with Li and muttered polite greetings. Then she walked over to the cart and shook hands eagerly with Wang, ceremoniously brushed the dust off Ling's shoulders, and took the little girl in her arms. The two women began to chat.

"Liang, come and say hello to your uncles," Li said to his son.

The giant Zhao Jialu picked Liang up before he had time to get out of the cart, enveloping him in an overpowering smell of tobacco. Liang looked at the faces around him. The voices were like a song whose tune he recognized without understanding the words, the echo of something that reached back to a time he could no longer remember. There were more faces than he could count, and they were all repeating the same refrain: "What a good little boy . . ." Then a voice seemed to sweep across the dusty plain and through the dim light, a voice that lifted him high. He tried to speak . . . "Uncles" . . . but could not. The voice was too strong, the song too sweet and soothing. "Uncles," he tried again to answer. The word rumbled inside him like a distant storm, like a river during the rainy season.

"Why don't you get settled," Zhao Jialu said. "We'll see to the rest later."

"Everything's arranged," Song said. "You'll live in the school where Sister Wang will teach. I asked them to set aside a corner room for you. It's quiet, and close to your work. You can get food from the teachers' canteen, so you won't have to cook much."

She took the donkey's bridle and led them toward the other end of the village.

Liang watched as his father shook hands with everyone

again, took the donkey's bridle from Song, and followed her down an alley near the church.

The welcoming voices were gone. It was dark now, and most of the village seemed to be asleep. The only sound was the donkey's hoofs echoing from the wall around the church. Liang wondered what was behind the wall that made the donkey sound so noisy. He looked up, suddenly wide awake. He saw pointed windows high above. The church seemed gigantic compared to the peasants' shabby houses. He felt afraid. What spirit lived in that dark place? Was someone watching them from behind those strange windows? Would that person come out, or would he stay inside forever, hiding in the darkness?

"The church is so big!" Liang said.

"Yes, it is," Song agreed.

She slowed down and took Liang's hand.

"It was built by the French. It used to be a church, but it's not anymore. Foreign reactionaries tried to poison us with religion, to make it easier to oppress us. We've turned it into the headquarters of the Party Committee. This is where we receive Party directives. The Revolution in the whole district is led from that building."

Liang tried to follow what the woman was saying in her authoritative voice. The words were familiar to him from his ethics class. The hand holding his had the same warmth as any other, yet something about it bothered him: she was squeezing hard, to the rhythm of her speech. "The church no longer exists," she said, and he felt three squeezes. It was annoying.

He made a timid attempt to get out of her strong grip, but she squeezed even tighter. It was too dark to see the face of this unknown comrade of his father's, so he tried to imagine the shape of her head, which seemed far away from the squat body that walked beside him. She had broad, swaying hips that rubbed against him as she walked. He could feel the warmth of her fat legs and smell her sweat.

Her legs, her hand gripping his, and her high-pitched voice were three enormous parts of a body invisible in the night. ". . . driven out . . . our glorious Revolution . . . the Great Leap Forward . . ." She kept talking. Her smell was too strong. Liang closed his eyes, then stumbled. A hand shook his shoulder.

"Wake up, little one. We're almost there."

"I'm hungry, Mama," Ling whined.

"It won't be long now," said her mother, who was walking behind, carrying her.

"Give her to me. You must be tired."

Song let go of Liang's hand and took the little girl on her back. "Ling is just as brave as her brother," she said. "Even braver. Because he's bigger than you. Yes?"

"Yes, Auntie Song," Ling said brightly.

So they already know each other, Liang thought. They must have been introduced while the men were talking. And Ling was never afraid of anything. She never stopped to think.

"What a good little girl!"

Song held her tight, and Ling gave a contented little laugh.

Liang, walking alone behind the cart, was a little afraid in the dark, but he was glad to be free of that grip, which his hand still felt. He uncurled his fingers and rolled his shoulders.

They passed some low houses. Against a faint reddish glow, shadows of people could be seen in the windows: a round head with a long-stemmed pipe; a woman, her hair in a bun, spinning; another woman, glasses perched on her nose, sewing. Scenes of people settling in for the night.

"You know, Sister," said Song. "You're from the town, where your life was very different from ours. You had everything one could dream of, but you gave it all up to come out here, in this remote outpost, to help Prefect Li make the Revolution with us. So I should consider you a part of my own family. Your difficulties are my difficulties. My mother is in good health, but she doesn't work in the fields anymore. If you want, I could ask her to take care of your little girl. I'm sure they'll get along well. Then you'll be able to work in peace."

"Ah," Wang said, "you really are my sister. I've been worrying about what to do with Ling. If Grandmother wouldn't mind taking care of my little one, it would be such a relief to us."

"We would pay her, of course," said Li.

"Don't they have kindergarten here?" Ling asked indignantly.

"Grandmother Song will be better than any kindergarten," Song said. "You'll see. She'll dress you in red, feed you pancakes, and tell you stories—revolutionary stories."

"I want to go to Grandmother Song's!" Ling shouted, clapping her hands. "I want her to tell me revolutionary stories!"

The cart stopped at an unlocked gate: the school.

In the large dusty courtyard some men were gathered around a lantern, whose flickering flame cast shadows on the building's ocher front. Song called out something, and two of the men hurried to pull open the double gate. Li began to unload the cart, as Song called the teachers, who lived in the school, to help the Li family move into the room assigned to them. It was in a back corner of the yard, overlooking a field of sorghum.

"You must be hungry, Prefect Li," said Song once the baggage had been carried in. "Let's go and eat. You can unpack later."

They went into the kitchen, a huge room with a floor of hard-packed earth. A dank, rancid smell choked Liang. He took a deep breath, inhaling a continent of new odors, and knew that they had truly arrived, and that they would be here a long time. He realized that he was very hungry.

When Liang went to bed after the long and tiring journey, after a day that had seen so many changes so hard to understand, he wanted to curl up quietly. The reassuring odor of the old cotton blanket he had used all his life comforted and relaxed him. Yet he felt he ought to draw at least a few conclusions from everything that had happened. He had to find some way to reestablish control over that boundless, secret part of himself that he rediscovered every night, as he lay in bed.

The long journey from their town to this wretched village was also a journey away from the person he'd been. It was an upheaval, as if the old, familiar habits of his daily routine had been lost. Now everything had to be rebuilt: the dreams and the images, the people and things around him, the rhythms of games and chores, of laughter and talk, the whole inner landscape of his body and mind. He was reminded of the ant hills he used to demolish with a stick in the courtyard of their house. The bewildered ants would run in all directions, like the thoughts that had run through his head today.

He was neither asleep nor awake. Deep inside him, hidden in the shadows, another self waited quietly, hoping to rescue him. His mother was right: he was not sleepy. But it was not because he had slept during the trip, or had pretended to. That was just to cover up his unhappy feelings, while his other self stayed peaceful.

He looked around this unknown room faintly lit by an oil lamp. It was his room now, their room. Two-thirds of the space was taken up by the big bed on which the whole family had to sleep. Liang's place was against the wall.

What was on the other side of the wall? Above, he could see a square window, through which the night and the silence poured in.

His mother would know what was on the other side. She was putting their things away. When she passed in front of the lamp, the room went dark; all he could see was her outline, ringed by a golden halo. He could ask her, but he liked to figure things out by himself. He could hoist himself up to the window and take a look. But then his mother would ask him what he was doing, in that sharp tone he hated. Her voice always grew sharp when he did something without asking permission first. So he thought it better to wait.

His sister lay sleeping beside him, making occasional little sucking noises. Probably dreaming of eating Grandmother Song's pancakes.

Liang closed his eyes and thought of Song, of her smell. He had just met her, but he was supposed to call her Aunt. She seemed nice enough, except for what she had done right after they'd eaten: she'd taken his father away on their very first night in this unknown place.

"Prefect Li," she had said, "we're going to have a meeting after supper, if you don't mind."

"Of course," Li had said. "We have so much to talk about."

But Li had hesitated. Liang knew that deep down his father did not want to leave his family alone, but no one else seemed to notice this. The Party and the Revolution always came first. Liang's parents had told him this more times than he could count. Without the Party he would have had no father, no family. So in the name of the Party, Liang had to accept his father's absence. Sadly and silently, he'd watched him go.

"When is Papa coming back?"

The question slipped out before he realized it.

"Probably very late," said Wang, stopping for a moment. She looked at him and sighed.

"Go to sleep," she said. "You have school tomorrow."

"I can't sleep," Liang said.

"You slept too much on the road. And it's a new bed. But try."

"Yes, Mama."

Liang kept quiet. Just outside the flickering circle of light around the lamp, a greenish shadow climbed from the bottom of the wall to the window frame. Blue and gray hung in the room. The night had no color of its own; instead, it swallowed all the colors. Liang stared intensely at the dark mouth of the window; tiny spots, broken lines, and shifting dust drifted back and forth. He saw the ruts in the road dancing by. When he closed his eyes and rubbed them, he saw showers of stars and strange round moons, which swooped and soared like dragon kites in a cobalt blue darker than any night.

"Liang, go to sleep!"

He sighed. Why did his mother always have to interfere just when things got interesting? She never said much in front of his father, except to agree. But with the children it was one reprimand after another: Go to sleep. You have to sleep because it's night, because there's school tomorrow, because tomorrow's another day, because, because, because . . . She had a million becauses. So did he, but no one ever paid attention to his.

Why had they left the town, where they were so happy? That Song woman said something about "making the Revolution." What did she mean? Hadn't his father already made the Revolution in their town? What would Liang's friends say when he didn't show up at school tomorrow? What friends would he have here? That little girl in red with the big yellow dog? Would the teacher be nice?

Liang couldn't think of a single thing he was sure of. There was no ground to stand on, no way to think about the future. He felt like a little tree that had been transplanted in a new hole. Now he was looking for a good piece of soil in which to put out his first root.

His mother still walked around. She seemed not to know where to put things. She stopped, holding one of Liang's jackets, then dropped it on a worn chair. She sat down near the lamp and began to sew. The light was so faint, she had to lean very close to see. Her shadow filled the room, covering Liang.

"How come we don't have electricity?" he asked, despite himself.

"They don't have it out here yet. But some day it will come."

Liang remembered the day the first electric light was installed in their house. His mother had cooked some wonderful dishes for the electrician. In the middle of the meal, his father got up, switched off the light, and turned on the oil lamp. "This is the weak light in which we have always lived," he said. "Today, thanks to the Revolution, thanks to the Party, we have this new light, this new happiness."

After that, whenever anything good happened, Liang said to himself, "Thanks to the Party." Maybe that was it. Maybe his father had to come here to help these peasants, for the Revolution.

"Why did we come here?" he asked aloud, surprising himself with the question. That's the way he was: only after first figuring out the answer himself did he dare ask the question aloud.

"Your father has been named assistant district leader," his mother answered softly.

"But this is just a village."

"That's true, and it's the poorest one in the district, and the hardest to administer. They needed someone the Party has confidence in. That's why your father was chosen."

The Party had more confidence in his father than in anyone else in the world! Liang smiled in the darkness. He remembered an argument between two school friends: "My father joined the Party before yours did." "But mine's a district leader." Now he could tell them both, "My father's the one the Party has most confidence in."

He began to hum softly a song his mother had taught him when he was very little:

> Let's sing for the Party.
> The Party is our mother.
> A mother brings a child into the world,
> But the Party lights up his heart. . . .

Just then he heard a voice in the night, outside. It was soft, near, deep.

Liang fell asleep.

A dazzling ray of sun, alive with dust, poured through the window and cast its sloping column of light into Liang's eyes. It reminded him of his loss, that the town and his friends were far away. That he was here—"thanks to the Party." It reminded him of the song, the Party's confidence in his father, the village . . . He felt very lonely. Your father, Prefect Li, is a hero of the Revolution, but you, Liang, no longer have your little bed. He sat up and looked at his father's empty place in the big bed.

"Didn't Papa come home last night?"

His mother was making breakfast.

"Of course he did. He left very early this morning. Come on," Wang said, laying some neatly folded clothes on the bed, "you have to get up too. Wear these. I want you to make a good impression in your new school."

Liang sat motionless, staring at his father's blanket, already neatly folded.

"Liang, get up," his mother pleaded.

She looked at him almost fearfully, he thought, as she filled a large bowl with rice. Liang pouted and gazed furtively at his mother, but quickly averted his eyes when she looked back. Grudgingly, he began to get dressed. He put one leg into his trousers and stopped. Out the window he saw a breathtaking view.

The furrows of a sorghum field stretched out under the rising sun like a joyous army with banners waving, or like a long green swell in a sea. The few huts scattered in the distance were like glittering yellow boats. Liang squinted and saw peasants emerging from the light, their plows drawn by yellow buffalo. Streaks of clouds cast a net from east to west, while glints of pearly sky shone through like fish caught in it. Closer, at the edges of the fields, weeping willows with twisted trunks waved gently in the morning breeze, beckoning him. Liang opened the window. Crisp air and the sound of birds swept into the room.

"Why are you playing with your pants like that?" Wang scolded.

Liang paid no attention. His left leg was still bare.

"What are you doing?" asked Ling, who had just waked up.

"It's really pretty outside."

"I want to see too," she squealed, trying to climb Liang's leg.

Liang took his sister in his arms and tried, without success, to lift her to the window.

"Stop it, both of you, or I'll punish you!"

His mother was angry now. Liang hurried to get dressed.

Maybe he was late. He heard children's shouts, tables and benches scraping the floor, and the voices of teachers: the usual sounds of the start of a school day. Excited by the noise, Liang washed his face hurriedly, grabbed the bowl of rice his mother had made for him, and wolfed it down in four gulps, almost choking himself. He was eager to go and join his friends. But then he remembered: he had no friends here; this was a new world. He would be going to school with villagers. The idea made his body stiffen as he remembered their small dark eyes staring relentlessly.

He pretended to be looking for something, stalling for time while he summoned up his courage.

"Don't forget this," his mother said, handing him his red scarf. "You have to make the right impression on the first day. That's important."

"Why is the scarf red?" Liang hummed as he stood in front of the mirror and tied it around his neck:

> *Why is the scarf red?*
> *Stained with the blood of the Revolution's martyrs,*
> *It is a piece of the red flag.*
> *We wear it, children of the Revolution,*
> *Heirs of Communism. . . .*

"Hurry up! You mustn't be late," Wang said, pushing him out the door.

In the courtyard, he saw a teacher waiting for him at the classroom door. He crossed the courtyard on trembling legs.

"Li Liang!" the teacher said, taking his hand. "Come. I'll introduce you to the class."

She led him to the platform at the front of the room. Liang stood with his head down, blushing with embarrassment, hearing only the beating of his own heart.

Then the introduction was over.

"You can sit down now, Liang," the teacher said, pointing to the only empty seat, which was next to a pale girl.

Liang finally forced himself to look up at the class. They were all staring at him. He hesitated, then shrugged his bag off his shoulders and started to sit down.

"No," said the little girl. "I don't want you next to me."

Liang looked at her. He had no idea what to do. She looked back at him, her cold eyes like two tiny triangles, her face in a pout.

"What's the matter?" the teacher asked.

"I don't want him next to me," the little girl repeated. Then she added, in an almost pleading tone, "Really, I don't. Or I'm going home."

The class was stifling its laughter. The teacher did not insist; instead, she sent two boys out to look for another table and bench for Liang. They left, and Liang took refuge in the back of the room. The boys returned with a pitted old table and a bench that didn't match. When they put them down, a leg gave way, and the table collapsed. The class laughed. Liang looked down at his feet.

The two boys kicked and hammered at the bad leg with a brick. Finally they managed to make it stay put. Liang sat down very carefully.

Class began. There were about forty pupils, divided into two groups, one that could already read and write a little and one that knew nothing at all. The teacher spoke to both groups at once. Liang felt alone among idiots. In his confusion, he kept seeing the expression on the face of the little girl who didn't want him to sit next to her. From where he sat now, he could see only the back of her neck and two little braids that shook with the movements of her head. The children around him were dirty; their manners were crude, their hair yellowish, dusty, their complexions pale, their arms and legs thin. He began to daydream, holding silent conversations with his friends in the town.

During the recreation period, he waited until everyone had left and then wandered over to the outdoor toilets. He was so disgusted by the holes dug into the ground, surrounded by low walls of packed earth, that he almost lost the urge. Big hairy flies buzzed in the excrement, and even their buzzing seemed to stink. He closed his eyes, held his breath, urinated as fast as he could, then backed out.

He was startled by a loud voice close behind him.

"Stop!"

He turned and saw a tall thin boy glaring at him. He tried to move away.

"Stop!"

The boy was one of the pupils in the second group, and had stared at him during the whole class period.

"Why?"

"What do you mean, why?" the boy said, coming so close that Liang could feel his breath.

The boy grabbed the red scarf, tugged hard at it. Liang was bewildered.

"What are you wearing this for?"

"It's . . . it's the red scarf of the Communist Young Pioneers."

The boy seemed not to understand. The red scarf angered him. His lips curled, his teeth were clenched.

"What's wrong?" Liang choked out.

"It's the mark of the Red Devil," the boy snarled.

"The Red Devil?"

"Yes, the enemy of God. I'm warning you: I don't want to see it tomorrow."

Suddenly Liang saw his mother crossing the courtyard, coming toward them.

"What are you doing?" she asked.

The boy let go of Liang and lowered his eyes, not daring to look at Wang. Liang saw that his hands were shaking.

"Playing . . ." the boy muttered.

"What's the matter?" Wang asked suspiciously.

"Nothing," Liang said. "We're just fooling around."

"Fooling around," Wang repeated, looking at the boy's hands, the crumpled scarf, and Liang's red neck.

"Yes, fooling around," Liang insisted, annoyed by his mother's intervention.

The boy gave him a glance of gratitude.

Wang looked at them again, sighed. "You should play nicely." She went back to her own class.

The two boys stood looking at one another. They were both relieved.

"Really," the tall boy said, "from now on you shouldn't wear that thing. The Red Devil . . ."

Liang gave him a puzzled look. The boy lowered his eyes and murmured, "Just don't wear it anymore. Because . . . well . . . it's very serious."

Liang somehow felt sorry for him.

The rusty old school bell gave out a grating sound like an old woman's voice made raw by too many hard years.

The two boys exchanged another look and went back to class.

五

Red, red, red . . .

The rusty bell rang again. Three times, slowly. The children ran off, shouting as though released from prison. Liang was left alone, the sound of the bell filling his head as though his skull was its rusty iron shell.

The sun, over the church steeple, was a red-hot iron disk lying on an anvil.

Red Devil . . .

Am I a thing that causes fear? Am I a Red Devil? Scorched trees, dried grass, yellow road, red devil, a rusty bell at sunset. What a strange land!

There was no one to talk to. Just a circle on the ground to hide in. Am I a thing that causes fear? Who will draw a circle inside me, a safe place the Red Devil cannot enter? . . . But the Red Devil is me . . . me.

Liang counted his steps. Head down, he took firm strides across the courtyard, leaving footprints in the dust. When he reached their room, he turned: he had made a perfectly straight path from the classroom door. Red Devil . . . Something flooded his chest and rose to his mouth like a too-hot swallow of tea.

The noise of the cicadas trapped him in the bright light of sunset. He didn't dare move. He felt empty, but he wanted to drive away the din of the screeching cicadas.

Liang spread his arms and threw back his head, squinting so that only the tiniest opening was left. Then he looked at the sun as it streamed through the leaves of a poplar in the courtyard. That was where the cicadas were. He went toward the tree, trying to step in his own footprints. The cicadas fell silent as he got close.

Standing in the sun in front of the tree, he yawned. It had been a hard day, with worry gnawing at his heart, but now he was free.

"Liang!" Wang called.

He retraced his footprints for the second time. It was cool in the dark room. He put down his bag and took off his scarf.

"Mama, what's a Red Devil?"

"Who mentioned a Red Devil?" Wang asked.

"Nobody." Liang sighed. "Well . . . at school."

Wang looked hard at him. "There's no such thing as a Red Devil, Liang," she said. "It's an insult that backward villagers use against us, against revolutionaries, Communists. Pay no attention to it."

There was a big green fly in the room, probably from that disgusting place.

"Nothing they say is true."

Wang opened the door to shake out a jacket. The hairy green fly flew out. Golden dust swirled silently around them before Wang closed the door again.

"Why did you take off your scarf?"

"It's too hot."

He was lying. It was not as hot as yesterday. It was almost cool. It must have rained somewhere.

"Did everything go all right in school?"

Liang did not answer right away. He knew he had to weigh every word when he spoke to his mother. Conversation with her was dangerous, full of traps. She saw right through what he said, because Liang was like a part of her body. Her body had made him, after all.

Her questions, his answers, and what she saw in them were a trail blazed into the depths of his heart.

"Not too bad. They aren't very smart," Liang said, pretending not to care and backing toward the door.

His hand was on the doorknob.

"Where are you going?"

"Out to play," Liang mumbled.

"Don't leave the school grounds. You don't know your way around yet."

"I won't. Anyway, there's no one to play with. I don't know anyone here."

Wang looked sharply at him, but said nothing. She went back to correcting her pupils' papers.

So it was that Liang left his mother on the evening of that first day in the village of Xin Zhuang.

Eyes half-closed, head turned up to the sky, he walked around and around the white poplar. The light sifted through the fluttering leaves and scattered on the ground like pearls strewn by Great King Sun, the Ape King. Thousands of magic pearls rained down from the Ape King's fingers. Liang had seen him in a movie.

"What do you want, little Liang? I am the Great King Sun. Tell me what you want, little Liang."

"I am afraid of the Red Devil, Great King Sun, Great Lord Ape."

"Go where you will, Liang, but do not step out of the circle I have drawn around you with my magic wand. Inside that circle the Devil can do you no harm. But if you leave it, beware! The Devil wants your flesh. He will eat you up! Then he will look just like you. 'It is I, Liang, son of

Li, son of Wang,' he will say. 'Go where you will, Liang, but don't leave the circle I have drawn around you with this magic wand,' "

Liang circled the white poplar, walking in the sun's footsteps, following the magic wand. Was his mother watching from the window? Better not go out; you don't know your way around.

He didn't know what to do. Keep walking around the tree. Maybe she would get tired of watching. Then he could slip out, take a look at that mysterious church with its arrow topped by a wooden figure ten.

He got dizzy, sat down. No one was watching. A cloud drifted across the sun, casting a shadow over the courtyard. The cicadas were silent. He picked up a stone and threw it at the poplar. A few leaves fell. His mother's words still echoed in his head. But what if he did go out? If he couldn't find his way back, all he had to do was ask. It was only a village, and there was only one school.

Red Devil . . . What if he ran into the tall thin boy? No, he didn't have to worry about that. He had taken off the red scarf, the Devil's mark. But what Devil was it?

"Don't leave the school grounds." As always, his mother's words were a wall that hemmed him in. "Disobey your parents, and you will live to regret it." That saying of Wang's had been drummed into his head a thousand times. Was the Ape King's magic wand a wiser rule?

"Is your mother home, Liang?"

A man's voice startled him. It was the young school principal.

"Yes, she is."

The man entered their room without knocking, and Liang heard him exchange greetings with his mother.

After walking around the tree again, Liang made for the

gate. There, with one foot on the threshold and the other in the road, he looked around to make sure he could beat a retreat if necessary. Then he went out, eyes wide open.

The village lay numb, deep in torpor. The houses, close together, seemed lower than they had before, deprived now of the mystery that the night had given them.

Just across the road, the pond they had passed last night looked filthy, a disgusting, murky yellow, like horse piss. Its surface was covered with water spiders that flitted back and forth on long crooked legs. The warm wind brought the smell of water left too long in a vase.

Liang, lingering at the gate, looked for the church, but his view was blocked by the house next to him. He took a few steps to skirt the wall, but hesitated again when he heard children shouting. Then he turned the corner and saw five or six boys about his age in front of the church, flapping their arms like eagles' wings. They were looking down at the ground as though chasing some animal, trying to make it run faster.

Cautiously, Liang moved closer. When he saw that the boy he was afraid of was not in the group, he walked toward them with more confidence.

The boys stopped playing and looked at Liang with suspicion, but their excitement soon had them shouting and waving their arms again. Ignored, he was able to watch them.

They held stacks of clay disks that left reddish streaks on their shirts. One end of a long brick leaned on a second brick to make an incline, and the boys were rolling disks down it, one by one. Each disk bore a figure in relief, a human or an animal from some old legend Liang vaguely remembered.

One was a woman in an old-fashioned dress, holding a child on each knee. She was Tin-Zhi, abandoned by her husband, who, when he was named prime minister, left her to marry the emperor's daughter. In the end, though, he had his head cut off, sentenced by the famous judge Black Bao, who appeared on another of the clay disks.

There was also an old man with a beard to his knees and a good-natured smile. He held a peach in one hand and, in the other, a crook with a handle shaped like a dragon's head. The God of Long Life, Liang thought, or something like that.

And there was King Sun, the Ape, with his golden wand that was capable of growing larger than the beam of a palace or shrinking smaller than a tiny needle which he could hide in his ear.

And the Horse and the Pig, the Ape's traveling companions, and the monk Tang, the Holy Man they followed on his pilgrimage to the West.

One disk rolled past the others. Chipped and worn, it wobbled but kept on going. Then it slowed, and finally stopped. With the sound of a dish shattering on stone, it fell and broke in two. On it was a snarling horned red devil, its long pointed teeth showing in its huge open mouth.

The player who had rolled it, a stocky boy with a shaved head and bull-like shoulders, cursed loudly, partly in anger, partly in triumph. He picked up the pieces of the broken devil, looked at them closely with tears in his eyes, then angrily tossed them away.

The players collected their disks and began another game. Shaved Head, the winner of the previous round even though his disk broke, went first. He took out a piece he had just won, the Ape, balanced it on the incline, and let it go. This time the disk, wobbling badly, didn't go nearly as far. It hit a pebble and fell, the Ape face up. The boy slapped his rear and groaned.

Liang was pleased at the boy's bad luck, though he was not sure why. Perhaps because the boy was so loud.

The second player, thin as a plant's stem, with very pale skin, stepped up. Liang heard the others call him White Face. His worn disk had filed edges, so it was rounder and smoother. It was the Boat and was apparently the one he used when he thought he had a good chance to win.

White Face stood behind the incline, sizing things up before he let the disk go. The Boat sailed swiftly on its way. He scurried beside it, singing softly and out of tune:

> Bobeel, Bobeel,
> Fine little wheel,
> Beat the Ape!

Liang had seen White Face give his disk a little push when he let it go, but he was glad the others hadn't noticed. He liked this pale imp with big cow eyes.

The Boat slowed and fell close to the Ape. Everyone ran to see which had gone farther.

"Mine, mine!" screamed Shaved Head, slapping his hands hard on his rear. "Mine went farther!"

"Like shit it did!"

"It did so, you little—"

"I won! My Boat won!" White Face said, shoving Shaved Head back.

The boys, after leaning carefully over the Ape, then over the Boat, unanimously declared the Boat the winner.

"Cheater!" screamed Shaved Head.

Liang went over and looked at the two disks. It was clear that the Ape had won, but he said nothing. He realized that the others had seen it too, but they had decided to let White Face win.

"What's wrong with you all?" Shaved Head shouted, his voice shrill. "You can see plain as day that my Ape went farther."

"It didn't!" White Face said. "The others said so!"

"Enough! I'll settle this," came a voice from behind Liang.

It was the tall thin boy, who had silently been getting ready to take his turn while the others were arguing.

His disk, Young Woman with Flute, sped as though he had thrown it instead of letting it roll down the incline.

"Out of the way!" he yelled fiercely.

But before Liang could move, the disk hit his left foot, bounced, whirled, and fell facedown. The back was a rough surface of dried mud with the maker's scrawled signature. Upset, Liang kept looking at the round piece of clay. It seemed like an angry person who had turned his back to avoid a fight.

"You did that on purpose!"

"I . . . I didn't," Liang stammered. "I didn't see it."

"Didn't see it, didn't see it! You don't see your mother piss either, do you?"

Liang, flushed, felt himself getting angry. He made a fist and looked Thin right in the eye.

"Who *are* you anyway?" Thin said, his head thrust forward, the veins in his neck sticking out. "I never saw you in this village before."

"If I had seen it . . ." Anger choked off the rest of Liang's words.

"It's true, he didn't see it," said White Face calmly.

Liang looked at him gratefully, but White Face seemed not to notice.

"If you don't see something," said a boy who had not yet taken his turn, "you don't see it." He was a good head taller than the others, and he had a man's voice.

"Where do you come from anyway?" asked a small boy with a reedy voice. "Don't you know you're supposed to get out of the way when people are playing?"

"Shit, he doesn't know. He's just as dumb as you are," said the big boy next to him, and he hit Small on the head.

"I have to lose my best piece on account of him," Thin whined, casting an imploring glance at Big.

"Well, I lost mine too," said Shaved Head. "Come on. Let's start over."

"No!" said Big. "What do you think this is?" He got ready to take his turn, glancing at Liang as though he were in league with him.

Liang suddenly felt unhappy. It was his fault that Thin would lose, and White Face too, who had been the first to stick up for him. And Small got hit on the head on Liang's account.

Big took his place at the incline. Legs apart, he took a very thick disk and placed it slowly, carefully on the brick.

Liang wanted only to get away from this circle in which fairy-tale figures mingled with crude peasant faces. Taking advantage of a new argument, he drifted back to the corner.

In front of him loomed the church, dark against the setting sun. A bird with a huge wingspan soared from the black steeple. It seemed to leave a wake of shadow behind it.

As he stood in the lengthening shadow of the church, Liang felt like a small island of fear in the sluggish river of sunset. He looked down at his bare feet in the dust. How he hated this dust! The tiny clumps of broken earth slipped between his toes as though they were all that remained of the fields, of the village. He shivered, feeling drawn to the dark shadow looming over him. He tried to raise his eyes, but found he could not.

"The imperial army marches out to meet the barbarian enemy."... What was he doing in this village? The boys and their shouts oppressed him just like the dust. Could he blow away from the village like the dust?...

Finally he looked up. The ten on top of the steeple reigned in the sea of clouds. Like a child before his teacher, he did not look at the church; the church, rather, looked at him, through the darkened eyes of its many arched windows, their wooden lattices all shaped like tens. A current of air came from the building's bulk, as though it breathed, and that strange-familiar breath drew Liang. A song rose inside him, a slow melody mingled with the beating of his heart. Why had they built those brick walls, pitted by wind and dust? Why did the walls climb so high over the earth houses, which stooped like old men under the weight of their masters?

Religion. Liang had heard the word before, but it had never meant much to him. The way his mother talked about it made him

六

see puppets whose strings were pulled by enemies of the people: sinister bandits, foreign spies, Western barbarians. He had never considered what religion actually meant.

What was the difference, for example, between God and the Great Lord of Heaven? The Great Lord of Heaven, wasn't he an ancient and honorable tradition of the people? So many questions . . .

It was strange. Liang felt as though some other being inside him were closing his eyes, drawing his eyebrows together, and making him frown, while he stood helplessly listening to his own questions. He summoned up his courage and raised his hand as if greeting the enormous building. No reply. The church seemed not to understand, or maybe it didn't want to. It stood motionless, resting confidently upon its great walls.

Just then Liang noticed something at the very top of the front, above a round window. It was the figure of a man carved in white marble. The thin, twisted body hung sadly on a huge ten. Scarlet streaks flowed from great nails that pierced his hands and feet.

Liang shuddered and looked at the high sunset sky. Around him now was deep silence. Who was that dead man hanging from the church? Why had they left him there, naked and in full view of everyone? Didn't they bury their dead?

"The wind of death shakes the grass and the trees."

Who had killed the man like that? Was he a bandit?

"The arrogance of the barbarians rouses the Emperor to anger."

Liang felt tickling in the soles of his feet and the hollows of his palms. He swallowed. His throat was tight. He had an urge to speak, but was afraid to disturb the inhabitants of this place, so close to the sky and so full of shadows.

Who was that man? Why had they hung him up there? Was it God, or the Great Lord of Heaven? If a god, he was certainly an unhappy god. Liang remembered the big portrait of Chairman Mao that hung on the wall of district headquarters in town. He remembered the affectionate gaze that followed you as you walked.

His mother had told him not to leave the school grounds. He would shrink when he faced her scolding look, her tenderness: "You can't fool me, Liang, I know you too well."

Shame pinched his heart. He hurried home.

In case the boys who had been playing had not gone away by now, Liang walked around the church, looking for an alley on the other side. He felt protected by the shadows of the walls, though the sky above was pale and desolate.

"Hey, look out!"

Liang flinched. A boy was sitting on the ground right in front of him, leaning against the wall. Liang had almost stepped on him. He smiled in apologetic embarrassment.

The boy, one eye open, the other closed, looked curiously at Liang. Two vertical lines went down his forehead. His hair was very long, closer to yellow then black, and it was parted on the right. Liang was not sure what to do, but for some reason he did not feel shy.

"I'm sorry," he said. "I was looking up at the building and I didn't . . ."

The boy didn't move or show any expression. Liang started to leave.

"You're Li Liang, aren't you?" the boy said.

"Yes. How did you know?"

"I know because I haven't seen you before," he answered in a high-pitched girl's voice. But he was sure of himself, like a man.

"You know everyone in this village?"

"Of course."

"Shaved Head and White Face?"

"Sure. I'd know those bastards even if they were burned to a crisp. Where'd you run into them?"

"I saw them playing."

"That clay-disk game."

"Yes."

The boy nodded, blinked like an old man, and said, "The stupidest game in the world. That's all they ever do."

"You don't like the game?"

"If you think it's interesting," he said, "that's only because it's new to you. Three days from now you'll be sick of it, believe me. You look smart."

"How old are you?"

"Me? Nine. You?"

"I'm nine too. My birthday's October tenth," Liang said.

"Mine's November ninth."

Liang sat down next to him.

"What's your name? You know mine, so you ought to tell me yours."

"Tian. Liu Tian."

"Why don't you like the disk game?"

"Because it's stupid." Tian shrugged with annoyance. "They win disks, lose disks, win them back, lose them again. They get a few disks ahead, but a few days later they're back where they started."

Liang thought about that. "So?" he said.

"So they ought to be doing something a little smarter. For instance, do you know what this is?"

Tian held out his hand and showed Liang a glass tube full of thin black needles. Liang felt a strange taste in his mouth.

"Let's see," he said, reaching out.

The boy pulled the tube away. "This," he said slowly, "is science. Do you know what science is?"

"Sure," said Liang. "Science is machines. The town's full of them. Trucks with huge engines that go really fast."

Tian looked admiringly at Liang, who had stood up and was waving his arms excitedly. Tian hesitated a moment, then asked, "In the town . . . is it true they have lamps that don't need oil?"

"Yes," said Liang. "It's called electricity. We had a lamp like that at home. So bright, you couldn't look at it."

Tian, his mouth hanging open, stared at him. After another silence, he held out the glass tube again and asked, "Well, can you tell me what this is?"

"Where did you find it?" Liang took a needle and examined it.

"In a wooden bucket behind the commune clinic. Where they throw the trash."

"I think," said Liang, frowning in concentration, "it must be for shots. When you're sick, the doctor gives you a shot. It really hurts. He takes a needle—a shiny one, made of metal—and sticks you in the rear. Then you're cured."

Tian watched dumbfounded as Liang did a quick imitation of getting a shot in the rear.

"Haven't you ever had a shot?" Liang asked.

"No. When I'm sick, my grandmother says a prayer."

"Who does she pray to?" Liang asked, curious.

"To the Lord of the Earth, of course," Tian answered, pleased at being able to teach his new friend something. "My grandmother believes in God—in this church, I mean. But she also believes in the Lord of Heaven. She says it never hurts to have extra Lords on your side. In other villages they only believe in the Lord of Heaven, but around here they believe in both."

"And what does the Lord of Heaven have to do with the Lord of the Earth?"

Tian, serious, spoke like a grownup. "The Lord of Heaven is the great master of all. He sends his servants to take care of things down here. The Lord of the Earth is in charge of what goes on in the villages, in people's homes. So when someone's sick, you have to pray to the Lord of the Earth."

Liang was fascinated. He hoped he'd see Tian again.

"Do you go to school?"

"Yes, but not every day," Tian answered gloomily.

"Why not?"

"Because I can't. When my mother works in the fields, I have to stay home and watch my little sister." Liang sighed with sympathy. "But it's the same with almost everybody in the village."

A gentle breeze rustled Tian's yellowish hair and blew a strange smell into Liang's face. He breathed it in and looked at the dirty boy sitting beside him. A sort of tenderness—a little mysterious, a little scary—swept over him.

It was late. He should go home.

"Why don't you come see me, and we can play," Tian said, his voice filled with hope.

"Oh, I will!"

"I live right over there, in the middle of that alley. The black door."

Liang looked where his friend was pointing. From the darkness by the church wall, he saw a very narrow black door, like a mouth full of secrets, waiting for its next visitor.

Liang felt a surge of happiness as he turned the last corner and saw, in their lighted window, a dark shadow: his father's shoulder. The sight of that shape, blacker than the night against the golden glow, sent a powerful emotion through him. All of his memories were now concentrated in Li's shadow, remote images of his life, freed of the limits of time and space.

One autumn, after supper, his father had hoisted him onto his shoulders, kicked open the door of their house, and gone out into the cool of the evening, bending so that his son's head would not hit the door frame. A blackbird was singing outside. Liang, jubilant, felt as though he were flying, soaring over mountains and gazing down into great valleys. The familiar household voices faded behind them; only the song of the blackbird stayed with them, surrounding them. The delighted Liang, giddy with the intensity of these new sensations, dug his heels into his father. Li's shoulders shook with laughter at his son's unexpected strength. The laughter bounced Liang up and down more quickly than the jostling of his father's walk. He dug his heels more into his mount's ribs. His father laughed again and began to run, brushing the branches of trees along the dark roads. Liang laughed too. Then, in a surge of excitement,

七

he squeezed his legs together with all his might, grabbed his father's hair, and screamed, "Stop! Stop!"

His father stopped, trying to catch his breath. The bird was still singing.

"Stop," Liang said again, and gave a final burst of laughter.

"Don't you want to run anymore?" his father asked.

"No," Liang said. "I just wanted to see how strong your shoulders were."

"A Party member," Li said, "has shoulders of steel. He can lift mountains."

Liang, dazed but reassured, fell silent.

Liang hurried to the door, anxious to see his father again, to tell him about all the things that had happened since he left the night before.

He ran in, without his usual knock.

The family was eating supper at the low table.

"You didn't listen, Liang," his sister said, putting down her little bowl and frowning at him. "You were bad. You'll be punished."

"Mind your own business," Wang scolded, not looking at her son hesitating in the doorway.

When Ling went back to her soup, slurping loudly, Liang took advantage of the noise to slip into his father's welcoming shadow. There he stood, head down, not daring to look at his parents.

"Well," said Li, handing Liang a bowl of corn mush, "what discoveries does our adventurer have to tell us?" The smell of the steaming food, mild and sweet, like his father's words, tickled Liang's nostrils.

"I made a friend."

"Good! And so soon," Li said in a playful tone.

"What's your new friend like?" Wang asked.

"Well, he's nice-looking. He's my age. And he likes science."

"What's that?" asked Ling in a voice that was part envy, part mistrust.

"Science," Liang said, raising his arms above his head, "is the most important thing in the world."

"Then I like science too."

Liang sat down and began to eat with as much noise as his sister. But then there was a knock at the door, two quick, sharp strokes. This surprised Liang. No one knocked like that in the town. When someone there came unexpectedly, the knock—soft, discreet—would herald a neighbor bringing a treat, or his father's secretary, or a friend. How different was this jarring sound, which emptied the room of its peace and brought something unknown, hostile.

Li got up, leaving his son without the protective shadow, and opened the door. It was Song. Her gray shape let in the night.

"Come in," said Li, "come in."

"Ah, I didn't realize you were still eating," said Song, taking a seat on the bed. "I came to tell you what went on in the Party cell today."

"Problems?" Li asked, assuming a serious official air. The tenderness he had shown a few moments before was completely gone. Liang stared at the woman, wondering how she had the power to take their father away.

"The big problem in this village is that the masses have not been properly awakened," the woman said slowly, in one breath. "Most of them are still mired in the poison of religion. They are still uneducated in loyalty and love for the Party."

Liang did not understand the rest. He watched her wide mouth open and close, her powerful jaw chew her words. At the end of each sentence her chin jutted out, showing its big wart. Liang looked away from it.

"I don't understand." His father's voice was slow, cautious. "How can they fail to realize that the Party has rescued them from poverty?"

"Of course," Song said hastily, extending her right hand and closing her fist nervously, as though trying to seize something invisible. "Before the Liberation, the people of this village were poor. Starving, in fact. There was no grain, the fields were barren, and there were droughts every year. The Party changed all that. The People's Commune organized the productive forces, and . . ."

Her jaw stuck out again, and Liang stared at the big wart that seemed to punctuate her words.

Song stopped in the middle of a sentence, her mouth open. Someone else had just knocked at the door. Wang went to answer. It was deputy secretary Zhao Jialu, followed by another member of the Party Committee. They, too, had come to report on the day's activities.

"Very well," said Li. "Let's have a meeting to go over all this: first the current situation, then the most urgent tasks."

Hastily gulping down what was left in his bowl, Li picked up his stool and sat down with Song and the two other Committee members.

Wang urged the children to finish eating and then to lie down on the bed and be quiet. Because she was not a Party member, she had no right to join the meeting. She tidied up the room and sat down to correct her pupils' papers.

"Perhaps Sister Wang should attend the meeting too, if she wants," Song suggested.

"No," Li replied. "It's important for us to set a good example of respect for the Party rules and discipline."

Liang lay in his spot against the wall, listening excitedly. This was a historic meeting. Though he was a mere child, he was being allowed to listen to the first Party meeting presided over by his father in his new post, a meeting not even his mother had the right to attend!

"Liang," Ling whispered, her eyes shining in the darkness, "do you want to play house?"

"Be quiet," Liang growled. How could she ask him to play some silly game when he had to concentrate all his attention on this special meeting?

Li declared the discussion open and immediately gave Song the floor.

"I am a child of this village," she began. "I was born here, I grew up here. And I can tell you that these people are backward, rooted in the most absurd superstitions and beliefs. If we want to apply Chairman Mao's revolutionary line in this district, the first thing we must do is weed out the most dangerous and disgraceful of these beliefs. I refer to the Christian religion. Only then can we hope to drum Communist thought into the heads of our unfortunate fellow citizens."

She stopped, looked around to check the effect of her words. Everyone nodded in approval. Li put his hands together as if in prayer and rested his chin on his fingertips. Silence.

Finally Zhao Jialu cleared his throat. They all turned to him. Song had a stubborn, self-satisfied look, a kind of half-smile, half-grimace. With her left eyebrow raised, she waited to hear what Zhao had to say, giving him the respectful attention due an elder.

"It's true," he said, and cleared his throat again. He had

a persistent dry cough. "Comrade Song is right. Religion is opposed to Communist doctrine. Those peasants who are still faithful to Christianity call us Red Devil."

He paused, rubbing the tip of his fleshy nose with his finger, as if sawing it.

"We can bring the people to Communism only by first destroying their religious belief . . . which is now quite strong. Let us not underestimate it."

Li said nothing. He smoked his cigarette with a superior air, as though weighing some decision, but secretly enjoying his position of power. As Liang watched, he was sure that he was the only one who knew what his father was thinking. Li had not spoken. He was the leader. It was only fitting that the leader let the others go first, that he listen to them carefully, because when he spoke, the Party, the Revolution, the cause of the Chinese people, even the cause of all the world's peoples would depend on his words. Yes, the fate of the world rested on those strong shoulders, shoulders Liang could climb onto whenever he wanted.

Li puffed his cigarette, still silent.

Then the third member of the Committee spoke. He was a thin man with a long face and almost transparent ears, which stuck out. His eyes, bloodshot, were half-closed. "I agree that we must struggle against religion. As we have always done. But the question is: What is the best way to wage that struggle? What measures can we take to wipe out beliefs that have existed now for more than fifty years and are rooted in the most ancient superstitions of our people? Has anyone come up with a solution to this problem? If so, let's hear it."

Song answered sharply. "We must never doubt the power of the Revolution, which will destroy all that is out-moded and backward. Communism is a positive force. Belief in religion is negative. Sooner or later, we will triumph. This conviction must be unshakable." She struck the bed with her fist, glaring at the thin man who had just spoken.

"You're right," said Zhao. "We must not doubt. If we have not yet triumphed, it is because we have not yet found the proper method. And perhaps also because I myself, one of those responsible for this struggle, am a man of insufficient wisdom. But now the Party has sent Prefect Li to our village. This gives us a great new opportunity to apply the Party line more effectively."

Zhao Jialu looked at Li as he spoke, as if trying to read his thoughts. Li ignored the compliment and waited for him to finish.

"We have the means at hand," said Song, "and effective means they are, too." Her eyes flashed as her gaze met Li's. "As I have said, the practice of religion goes on in secret. We must expose it. If we catch the ringleader and reeducate him, the religious movement will cease to exist." Leaning forward, her left hand clutching the blanket, she spat these words out as though they burned her mouth.

"That is for Prefect Li to decide," the old man said, and turned to him, as if beseeching.

Li did not speak immediately. A match crackled in the silence as he lit another cigarette. He shook it out.

Liang felt the tension. He set his jaw, then sighed and nodded, as though he were the one making the decision.

Finally Li broke his silence. "Comrade Song has spoken wisely," he said. "I share her view, and yours." He spoke slowly, weighing his words, as a leader must. Liang savored every syllable, repeating them softly to himself, like a prayer.

"Yes, we must destroy these beliefs, we must root out religion—of that there is no doubt. . . . Yet this is not the most urgent thing. First, we must see to it that the people understand why the Party is good, why they must love it. Now, why must the people love the Party? Because it brings happiness, because it helps them to surmount the trials they suffer. And what is the greatest trial today? Drought! That is the enemy we must defeat if we are to convince the people. As Comrade Song said, this was once a very poor region. Is it rich today? To me, it looks as poor as ever. If we want the people to love us and believe in us, we must help them become richer. How? By producing more grain. Anyone can see how the land suffers because of this drought that parches the fields. The drought is the first thing we must combat."

The decision was made. Liang's eyes filled with tears of pride. "Thank you, Papa. We have won," he murmured, relaxed and happy, as if he had just accomplished some great feat. Triumphant, he looked at the Song woman's back. She had been so vehement just a little while ago, but now she was silent. Yes, Liang thought, she's right. We have to fight religion. But she's not in charge around here. It's the leader who decides what the struggle should be, and the leader is my father. He says the fight first has to be against . . . What was it? Liang could not remember, but that didn't matter. The main thing was that his father had spoken, and that he had won.

"Prefect Li is wise," said Zhao Jialu. "We must struggle against the drought, and once we have conquered it, once the peasants' granaries are full, then they will listen to us."

"Yes," said the other man. "I, too, was born in this commune, but in another village. In the old days my father had a plot of land. There was a great drought. My father dug a well, and we irrigated our land with well water. That way we were able to survive when everything around us was parched and dead."

"There!" said Li, slapping his hand on his knee. "That is what we must do. Tomorrow morning we will begin mobilizing the commune to dig wells. We will draw up a plan. One well for every fifty square yards, dug by teams of two. Each team will dig one well a day. All the Party cadres will participate too, including us."

"And the women," said Song, her voice shrill. "I'll organize them. The young ones who are strong enough will work like the men, and the others can prepare food and carry it out to the workers in the fields. We'll make red flags and put them up at the wells. One well, one red flag!" Song turned red herself.

"An excellent idea," said Li, standing up.

Liang listened to their talk from his dark corner without understanding all of it. It was like a play, when the hero has won, and the audience, applauding, no longer hears him.

But was Liang actor or spectator, hero on the stage or someone in the audience? He saw himself laughing, digging wells, carrying water, irrigating sorghum plants in the sun. A Red Devil, a conqueror . . .

He fell asleep.

Whatever you do, keep walking, don't look back. Liang was already far from the school's gate, which glared like a wide-open eye. He walked with a determined stride past the proud church, which seemed annoyed by its immobility. It was Sunday, a free day, at least for him; his mother had to go to a meeting. He was setting out on a new adventure, and this time he had permission, more or less.

"While I'm gone," Wang had said just before she left, "you stay here and finish your homework."

"What do I do after that?"

"Why don't you read?"

"All right. And after that?" Liang's voice shook.

Wang looked at him and sighed. "If you go out, make sure you're back in time for supper."

"Of course," Liang answered in his grown-up voice.

Wang hesitated, apparently regretting what she'd said. "There's money in the drawer," she added. "You can take some."

Who could ask for anything better? Liang did his homework in ten minutes, took a book and left it open on the table, then went out. He crossed an alley and turned the corner near an old house. His legs felt a little unsteady, not out of fear, but from anticipation.

He came to a bigger street, deserted in the late-morning sun. A hot, dry wind shook the leaves of a poplar, which groaned in pain.

54

Ahead, under a dirty white awning at the entrance to another old house, Liang saw a strainer made of willow branches hanging from a red ribbon. Drawing closer, he saw that this was a teahouse. He peeked through the open door and saw a few worn chairs and two tables of white wood covered with black grime. There were also dusty spiderwebs and a terrible smell.

"You want something to drink?" asked a voice that sounded like the sudden clearing of a blocked drain. It belonged to a thin old man with lifeless eyes and a quivering white beard.

"No, thank you, Grandfather," Liang said, feeling in his pocket for the two five-fen coins he had brought with him from home.

"Too bad." The old man's jaw moved under wizened skin. There was a sharp creak when he sat down on his bamboo stool. It was hard to tell whether the noise came from the bamboo or from his stiff joints.

"Whose child is that?" asked another voice, scratchier than the first. It came from a corner of the teahouse. Liang saw two old men sitting at a table drinking tea. Their thin bent backs made them look like giant shrimps. The rags they wore left much of their skin exposed, which, sunburned, made them look as if they'd been fried in the huge pan of life. Clutching their teacups with twisted fingers, they exchanged vacant glances, their mouths trembling as though they were pondering problems that had no solution. Otherwise they were nearly motionless; they might have been sitting there since the beginning of time. Their eyes were filled with boundless self-assurance.

"Doesn't look like a boy from this village," remarked one of the three living dead.

"Probably the new prefect's son," the owner of the tea-house said.

"Oh, is there a new prefect?" the third old man asked, turning toward Liang without opening his eyes.

They moved closer together and began to whisper. The breathless hum of their voices merged with the sound of simmering water.

Liang couldn't hear what they said, but a moment later they burst into a roar of raucous laughter interrupted by explosive coughing.

Suddenly noises came from the alley. Liang looked and saw four or five children, nearly naked, crouching around an old man with a gray beard. Going closer, Liang saw that the old man was making little figures out of dough. His dirty fingers, like clusters of dried nuts, moved quickly and skillfully. He stuck a red piece on a green piece, creating an elegant dress. A yellow piece was added for the head. With a tiny knife, barely bigger than a needle, he carved a mouth and nose and dug out two eyes. It looked like a real person. The children took it, played with it, then ate it.

"This Little Lord Son looks as though he might have some money. How would you like a whole set?" the old man asked Liang, pointing to a group of different figures in old-fashioned clothes. Liang counted seven men and a woman. They had strange faces.

"Who are they?"

"You don't know?" the old man asked in astonishment at such great ignorance. "They are the famous eight gods. There's an old saying: Eight gods cross the sea, each showing his power. See, the gentleman with the black face is Tie Guai Li, who burned the sea to save his companions from the dragons' jaws. The beautiful lady in the red skirt is He Xiangu, the aunt goddess who charms everyone. Black

Beard over there rides his donkey backward. The one with the dog is Lü Dongbin."

The old man introduced all eight characters, recounting the exploits of each. Excited by these ancient legends, Liang decided to buy the figures. He handed over his two coins.

"Don't forget, Little Lord Son," the old man said as Liang turned to leave, "the dough is sweet."

Just then Liang heard a man singing in another alley. He hurried around the corner and saw a peddler selling cloth, surrounded by three old women.

"Let me see that black piece," said a woman with a child in her arms. The peddler, who wore a ragged straw hat, tossed her a piece of cloth. As the woman examined it carefully, the peddler, his eyes half-closed, began his refrain again with a mocking air:

> *Why so black, so black?*
> *Three years a blacksmith,*
> *Three years a chimney sweep,*
> *And three years more in the mine.*
> *That's why it's black, so black. . . .*

"Could you let me see that white piece?" asked another woman, a newcomer. The peddler handed her some cloth and sang:

> *Why so white, so white?*
> *A young bride, just from her mother's,*
> *Never goes into the courtyard,*
> *Never crosses the threshold;*
> *Sheltered from wind,*
> *Sheltered from sun.*
> *That's why it's white, so white. . . .*

The peddler sang, the child fell asleep, and the women finally bought the black cloth, the white cloth.

Liang stayed and watched, captivated by the peddler's song, his melancholy, faraway voice. Liang felt that he had fallen into a long-ago and mysterious age inhabited by wondrous characters: the Ape King, the eight gods, a man all black, a great blacksmith with a wild beard.

The sun beat down more strongly. Liang thought it must be noon. His stomach growled. All he had were the eight little dough figures. He ate them.

I'm the red-eyed monster that devours children, he thought, twitching his tongue.

He walked around to the other side of the church, remembering Tian's directions, and found the black door. Full of little holes and scratches, it looked as if it had been closed forever. As he stood there, thinking the door might lead straight to hell, it opened with a loud creak.

A man stood there. "Looking for Liu Tian?" he asked.

He was broad-shouldered, with a serious face, round eyes, and a thick beard and eyebrows.

"Yes," Liang answered timidly. "Is this his house?"

"It is," the man said. "I'm his father." He turned and shouted, "Tian! Your friend is here to see you!" Then he turned back to Liang, smiled, and said, "Well, I'm off to the fields."

Tian came skipping across the courtyard, took his friend by both hands, and pulled him in.

The courtyard of the Liu family's house was round and not very big. An old jujube with a gnarled trunk, some fruit already showing among its green leaves, stood in the middle. On the west side was a cowshed, where a large pig was feeding. A few chickens pecked at the pig swill. Off to the other side, a big white goat was tied up.

"Grandmother," Tian called, his eyes full of kindness, "this is Li Liang, my new friend."

The door of the old house rattled, and a wrinkled face appeared.

"Hello, Grandmother," said Liang.

"These are good days. The days are always good . . ." the old woman said. She looked carefully at Liang, opened her toothless mouth, and asked, "Is your father the new prefect?"

"Yes," said Liang, feeling self-conscious.

"What a nice boy! What a good-looking boy!" she said. "I'm not surprised. There's an old saying: Only to a general's family can a general be born."

While Grandmother Liu stood there humming to herself, Liang entered the house with Tian. Like all peasant homes, it had three rooms: a bedroom at each end and a room in the middle that served as a kitchen. The house was low, and it was stifling.

"Do you want to go out?" Tian asked, wiping sweat off his own face and off Liang's.

"Oh, yes."

"I was going to take White out to graze. We can go together."

"Tian, my boy," his grandmother called out, "bring me straw. I want to heat some water for our future prefect."

"No, don't bother," Tian said. "We're taking White to the fields."

"What? You can't do that!" said the astonished old woman. "You can't let him go to the fields. He's the prefect's son."

"Oh, Grandmother," Tian drawled, "things aren't like that anymore."

"He's right, Grandmother," said Liang, trying to sound

like his father. "My father and I both serve the people. He works in the fields too."

Tian took his friend by the sleeve and said, "Let's go."

Tian's grandmother was muttering as they left. "It's not right, a prefect working in the fields! What an age we live in, what an age! The chief doesn't look like a chief anymore, and the feet wander where they will. Terrible!"

Tian and Liang went out into the courtyard and untied the goat, which was almost as big as a calf. It bleated and pranced. Liang held White's tether, and Tian carried a basket on his shoulder. They headed out of the village as a big cloud temporarily covered the sun, and the wind seized the opportunity to blow harder. It was a pleasant summer afternoon.

As they walked along the high church wall, Liang suddenly asked, "What's inside?"

"Inside the church? God," Tian answered without thinking.

"What does God look like?"

"I don't know much about all that," Tian murmured, shrugging his shoulder to balance the basket, which was too big for his scrawny body.

Liang looked at him in surprise. How could you live right next to something for so long and know nothing about it?

The goat, impatient, pulled ahead of the boys. Liang had to run to keep up with it.

"Your mother's not home today. How come they allow you out?" Liang asked.

"My mother's working in the fields, like my father. They're digging wells. But guess what." Tian was obviously delighted. "I'll be able to come to school every day now.

They've started a nursery here, and my parents put my little sister in it."

"You'll really be coming every day?" Liang asked, pleased.

"Yes. Don't you know about it? It was your father who gave the order."

"My father?"

"Yes. Everyone in the village is saying nice things about your father."

"Oh, yes, now I remember. There was a meeting in our room the other day, and I heard my father say something about wells, but then I fell asleep." Liang spoke gravely, as if he had given the order himself.

"Anyway," Tian said, taking Liang's arm, "thank your father for me."

Liang nodded, though unsure if he was permitted to accept thanks on behalf of his father.

They left the village. Ahead of them stretched a broad plain studded with hills that looked like loaves of corn bread. The fields shone green, and red flags fluttered everywhere as peasants moved among piles of fresh dark earth.

Looking upon the scene, Liang felt even prouder of his father, the hero, the savior of the people, the only representative here of the beloved Party. Grandmother Liu's phrase rang in his ears. "Only to a general's family can a general be born." Liang held his head high and threw his shoulders back, gripping the goat's tether like the reins of a war-horse. He strutted, feeling the weight of great responsibility on his shoulders.

"Careful!" Tian shouted. "You're strangling White."

"Oh . . . sorry."

They came to a fork in the road. "Which way do we

go?" Liang asked loudly, trying to hide his embarrassment.

"Just let White go. He knows the way."

The goat, pricking up his ears, unhesitatingly took the more winding road. The boys followed closely after him.

"That's a smart goat," Liang said.

"Sure is. He knows all the roads back, too."

"Have you always had him?"

"No. Just this year," Tian explained. "We do the same thing every year. We kill the goat and the pig for the spring holiday. Then we raise another goat and another pig for the next spring. . . . This year we're killing the pig early, because my sister's getting married."

"When?"

"In three or four days . . . Listen, why don't I ask my father if you can eat supper with us tonight?"

Liang squeezed Tian's hand and gave a little jump of joy.

They came to a hillock, where the goat began to nibble fresh grass. A sweet smell came from its mouth. Liang picked a stem and also began to chew. Tian knelt down to cut grass to carry home in the basket.

As a big cloud drifted by and cast a blanket of shade over the fields, Liang tasted the juice of the grass and flared his nostrils to let the freshness fill his lungs.

Tian began to sing:

> *Why are we born? To serve God.*
> *We suffer much, but God forgives.* . . .

"What's that song?" Liang asked.

"I don't know, but my grandmother sings it a lot. I learned it from her. Do you like it?"

"Yes."

Tian sang on:

> *We serve God, and when we die,*
> *We go to paradise. . . .*

He sang off-key, in a childish voice. The melody was too soft for a man's heart, too plain for a woman's. But Liang felt his heart dissolving into a thousand pieces, which were carried through his bloodstream to his fingertips, his toes, even his hair.

Without thinking, he began to sing along with his friend.

> *We serve God, and when we die,*
> *We go to paradise. . . .*

九 The chittering of the cicadas seemed to make it even hotter. Not a single leaf stirred.

Liang was bored. Sitting in the back row at a table that let out a squeal whenever he touched it, on a bench that creaked whenever he moved, he hunched his head into his shoulders and yawned. He yearned for the end of this lesson, but it had only just started. He wasn't the least interested in politics. The principal used the same slogans in every lecture; he expected his pupils to show proper discipline, liking the ones who sat stock-still and never said a word, detesting anyone who expressed an idea that was the slightest bit out of the ordinary.

Liang had been criticized twice for reporting news that the principal had not yet heard. "Don't think you know everything just because you're the prefect's son," the principal had said in front of everyone. "The Party's decisions are confidential. Not even your mother has the right to hear them in advance."

Liang blushed with shame; he knew the young man was referring to the fact that his mother was not a Party member.

"Why is our Party great?" the principal asked. "Because," he answered himself, "it forbids private relationships. All affection is class affection. We love one another because we are all of the proletarian class. If you do something wrong, you will be punished just like everyone else, even if you *are* the prefect's son. In fact, if your father has something official to say to your mother, strictly speaking he ought to tell me first; it would then be my job to tell it to her. And with you, the procedure would be even more complicated."

Liang felt disgraced when the pupils laughed. He hated the principal after that, hated the lessons in politics even more.

"Li Liang!" the young man called out.

"Yes." Liang, absorbed in his own thoughts, saw a question written on the blackboard as he came back to reality: What is a Young Pioneer?

"Would you like to tell us something about this subject?" the principal asked in a strange voice.

"Yes . . . all right," Liang stammered, feeling himself blush. "In our town, I was one." Now he had the chance to talk about something no one in this village knew anything about. He had been a Young Pioneer, and they accepted only the best pupils. It was from their ranks that the Party drew its recruits.

"I was one . . ." But Liang could not think of anything else to say.

"Yes," said the principal. "That's why I want you to tell us a little about it. As I just said, we are planning to form a unit of the Young Pioneers here in our school."

This news started Liang daydreaming. If they did set up a unit, he would be the first to join, he would probably be the leader. What an opportunity! His father the head of the district, and he the head of the children! Grandmother Liu was right, a general's son is always a general. Liang could imagine how pleased his mother would be, and how proud his father would feel.

Excited, he repeated what he had learned when he first joined the Young Pioneers. He groped for words that refused to come, but somehow or other he managed to speak.

At the end, he raised his fist straight over his head as his fascinated classmates watched. "That's how we salute each other," he explained. "It's also a sign of being comrades—because we're all comrades."

The principal then continued his instruction.

Liang, however, paid no attention. Instead, he was picturing a beautiful autumn sunrise, a crimson sky, the smell of corn, his comrades lined up in formation, dressed in white shirts and blue trousers, red scarfs fluttering at their necks. He saw himself standing in front of the group, issuing orders. He had three red stripes on his left armband, the insigne of the leader. . . .

The sky grew dark with roiling black clouds, and an angry wind tore at the trees. The enemy lurked in the shadows, looked at the village with hungry eyes. The Red Army was still far away, fighting a bitter battle. The innocent masses in the village were unaware of the danger. Grandmother Liu was sleeping, holding Tian's little sister in her arms. The goat White knelt in the courtyard, eyes closed, chewing slowly, his head moving slightly, like that of an old man pondering a puzzle still not solved. Ling was also in the dream, soundlessly moving her lips. His mother finished correcting her papers and prepared the next day's lesson; then she lit a cigarette and propped her head in her hand. Leaves whispered, crickets played.

All this would be laid waste by the enemy soldiers, who were creeping up like wolves and training their rifles on the glowing windows.

A boy wearing a red scarf and carrying a spear in his hand galloped up to report to Liang, who listened gravely. Binoculars hanging around his neck, Liang paced back and forth with his cloak draped over his shoulders, calculating the enemy's firepower, the time it would take to evacuate the masses to the mountains, the risk involved in launching an attack before the Red Army came. Then he announced his decision, in a tone as solemn and resolute as his father's when his father spoke of the struggle against the drought.

Liang's mind was a jumble of images and words as he sat stiffly at his wobbly table. He blinked, frowned, folded his hands, wiggled his thin legs. It felt good to imagine himself a hero, a man of power, famous, praised by all.

He did not hear a word the principal said. The principal was saying: "The Party Commune Committee has decided that the main enemy of Communism in this district is the practice of religion. The main task of anyone aspiring to membership in the Young Pioneers is to struggle resolutely against religion."

How should he approach his mother? Would she agree? If she didn't, what could he do to convince her?

It took twenty-six and a half steps to go from the classroom to the door of their room, and Liang had to find some answers in the last twelve steps. He quickly reviewed the situation. He and his family had arrived here only recently. This would be the first time for him—a mere boy of nine, or nine and a half to be exact—to go out alone at night. His mother might say no, nicely but firmly. Then what?

Liang would be smart, like a man; he would make his mother treat him like a grownup and give him permission. Maybe the best way was to start casually by bringing up something else, get her talking about what he did that was good, his schoolwork for example. Then she would find it hard to say no.

But as it turned out, it was his mother who spoke first: "The principal says you did very well the other day, when you told your classmates about the Young Pioneers. You made a good impression."

Wang stopped and looked suspiciously at Liang. "What's the matter?" she asked.

"The matter?" said Liang, lowering his eyes. "Nothing."

"Yes. Something's on your mind. Tell me," Wang insisted.

Liang looked at her, then glanced away

again. He grunted without opening his mouth; the sound came through his nose.

"Come on, what is it?" his mother said quietly.

"Well . . . tonight . . . I might not be eating at home," Liang stammered. "I've been invited . . ." He was angry the moment he said it. Why had he blurted it out so quickly, so clumsily? Why hadn't he tried to work his way around to it?

"Who? Tian?"

"Yes. I mean, Tian's father."

"Why?"

"Well, Tian's sister's getting married tomorrow, and they're having a sort of family supper tonight, so he invited me. I don't really want to go, because, of course, I have homework to do. But he said I wouldn't be home late. I tried to tell him I don't go out at night because I don't know my way around yet. But he really wants me to come, and he said it isn't far, and so I . . ."

Liang stopped. His mother wasn't listening. There was a noise outside. By some miracle, Li had come home early.

"Are you eating with us tonight?" Wang asked, beaming.

"I can't," said Li. "I have urgent business in Fan Zhuang, a village about ten kilometers from here, and—"

"It's more like fifteen," Wang interrupted in a tone of reproach.

"Ten, fifteen, what's the difference?" Li answered gruffly, slouching a little. "I have to be there by sundown. I came home to tell you and to pick up some corn bread to eat on the way."

"Well," said Wang, "if you have to, you have to. Men always seem to come up with good reasons not to stay home—even this small son of yours."

"What do you mean?"

"He's been invited to dinner at Liu Tian's tonight."

"Oh, good," Li said, looking at his son.

"Tian's sister's getting married tomorrow, and they're having a big meal tonight," Liang explained. "They're going to kill the pig like it was spring holiday."

"Tian's father is Liu Zhen Hua, isn't he?"

"Yes."

"Let's let him go," Li said to Wang after a moment's thought. "The Liu family has a good reputation. And it wouldn't hurt for Liang to get to know some people on his own."

"Mama, you know I always do my schoolwork," Liang said, looking at Wang with pleading eyes.

"You're spoiling this boy," Wang murmured, frowning at her husband.

"Hurrah, I'm going!" Liang shouted triumphantly. He bounded out the door.

"Don't be home late," his mother called after him.

He had just turned the corner into Tian's alley when he heard the squealing of the pig. The sound stung his ears, nose, eyes, pricked the soles of his feet, the palms of his hands, and it clawed at his legs. He broke into a run, not to get there faster, but to shake off the sound.

As he went through the black door into the courtyard, the pig, lying on a low table with its legs tied, squealed louder, as if calling to Liang for help. Standing beside Tian, Liang saw an old man with no shirt, his chest covered with hair, who was sitting in the doorway sharpening a knife on a big stone.

"This is my grandfather," Tian said.

The old man turned toward Liang and smiled warmly, without stopping his work. "You're Tian's friend?" His voice was raspy, probably from alcohol.

"Yes, Grandfather," Liang answered.

The old man said no more. The boys watched his broad, bronzed, and muscular back as he worked.

"My grandfather's the one who's going to kill the pig," Tian explained.

Liang looked at the sharp knife as the old man slapped it back and forth along the stone, stopping regularly to dip it in water. The knife squealed too, though more faintly than the pig. The pig's little pink eyes were also watching it. The pig no longer squealed—maybe it was exhausted. Instead, it groaned in a shaky, desperate voice.

"It's crying," Liang said softly to Tian, pointing at the pig.

The pig's voice suddenly got louder and shriller.

"Don't point," Tian said. "Pretend you don't see it. Otherwise it'll scream louder."

"But it's crying," Liang repeated, turning away. He felt a pain in his stomach.

Tian's grandfather shook his head. "No, pigs can't cry. They're animals without feelings. All they know how to do is squeal. They squeal when they're hungry, when they're thirsty, when you pet them, and when you kill them. Whatever you do, they squeal in the same way."

He glanced briefly at Liang and went on, as if he thought the boy was not convinced: "You should think of them as meat, not people. Otherwise you can't do anything with them."

He finished sharpening the knife, put down the stone, and carefully felt the cutting edge with his big rough fingers.

He wiped some spots off the knife, which now shone brightly, and held it up to the fading daylight to examine it more closely.

Liang's heart was pounding as he asked his friend, "Is your grandfather a butcher?"

"Oh no. He's the village pottery master. We can go watch him work someday."

Grandfather Liu, holding the knife behind his back, strode toward the pig, which watched him wide-eyed, chops pulled back, revealing yellow teeth. The squeals were unbearably piercing now. The old man circled the animal and nodded slightly, as though thinking hard before making a decision. "Go get a large bowl and call your father," he finally said to Tian. "Time to start."

Tian ran into the house, and came back with a large clay bowl. Liu came out too, rolling up his sleeves as he walked. The four of them stood around the pig. Grandfather Liu put the bowl under the animal's neck.

Liang could not take his eyes off the old man's hands, but his legs trembled, and through his body he felt a surge of revulsion. His heart was still pounding as though he were himself a wild animal gripped by the fear of death. Yet he also felt a thrill of curiosity.

"Can you give us a hand?" Liu asked Liang.

"All right," Liang murmured.

"You and Tian hold the back legs. I'll take care of the front ones."

The pig bellowed as Grandfather Liu, holding the knife under his arm, spat loudly into each hand. He grabbed the pig's snout with his left hand and pulled its head back, completely exposing the black neck. The neck, Liang saw, was the softest and most vulnerable part of the animal; the hair was thinnest there, the skin smoothest. The neck throbbed to the rhythm of the pig's squeals.

The old man held the knife in his right hand and placed it in the middle of the quivering flesh. Slowly the blade began to sink in. It sliced cleanly. The animal's shrieks were deafening, its struggle desperate. Liang and Tian had to use all their strength to keep their grip on the twitching, thrashing legs. Liang felt like closing his eyes when the blood spurted, but he found he could not. An unknown force held them open, and a wave of dizziness swept over him.

Grandfather Liu pressed the knife into the pig's neck with all his strength. The squeals became a rattle, and bubbling blood gushed into the bowl. Liang thought he could hear another sound beneath the pig's cries, the grating of metal on bone.

The animal groaned less and less, as though it were falling asleep. The blood had almost stopped flowing, and the leg Liang held seemed to go slack.

"We have to empty out all the blood, or the meat will go bad," said the old man, and he began to twist the knife.

More blood flowed, and the animal, roused by this new violence, struggled with its last ounce of strength. Liang felt his hands tiring and was about to let go, when suddenly Tian released the leg he was holding. Liang, unable to hold on alone, let go, and Liu jumped on the pig to keep it down.

"What's the matter?" Liang asked his friend, who was sitting on the ground.

Tian did not answer.

"Don't speak to him," Grandfather Liu ordered.

Then Tian gave a terrifying scream, as loud as the pig's had been, as though he were the one being killed.

"Go! Get out of here!" the old man yelled, angry.

"Take him outside and play for a while," Liu whispered to Liang.

Liang took Tian's hand and led him to the street.

"What is it? What's wrong?" he asked when they were outside.

"I don't know . . . I'm not sure," Tian mumbled. He opened his eyes wide in the darkness of the night. He groped for words. "My head's spinning. But you—your hands are shaking."

"Yes . . . and my head's spinning too," Liang said.

The two friends were silent for a while. At last they looked at each other and smiled, though neither knew why. Liang saw tears in his friend's eyes.

"Do you want to go and watch the games in the street?" he asked, to change their thoughts.

"Games in the street?" Tian seemed not to understand.

They could not hear the pig squealing in the courtyard anymore. It's dead, thought Liang, squeezing his friend's hand.

By the time the boys got back, festive red streamers had been hung everywhere. The whole Liu family had gathered, and friends were arriving to congratulate Ying, Tian's older sister.

The pig that had been squealing so loudly not long ago had been turned into chunks of red meat on earthenware plates. Tian and Liang were invited to sit in the western room, the larger one, which was reserved for the men. About twenty young men were already at the table, drinking noisily and issuing sly mocking challenges to make their companions drink even more.

"It's like this," said one, holding out a full glass. "Our sister's wedding will be the only holiday of her life. If I don't take this opportunity to offer Cousin Number Three a drink, I'll never be able to look my sister in the eye again."

Cousin Number Three, already tipsy, took the glass in a shaky hand, but, instead of draining it, he set it down on the table, picked up a piece of meat with his unsteady chopsticks, put it in his mouth, and then spoke as he chewed. "You're right, Old Fourth. Today is not a day like any other; it's a time for drinking. But excuse me if I don't drink this glass of yours. The trouble is, it's so tiny. We've been drinking for more than an hour now, and you might think I've had too much. But I'm nowhere near drunk. The truth is, it's been like drinking out of a

十一

bird's cup. That's not very respectful of our sister, who's gone to so much trouble for us, is it?"

He stopped to swallow his food, then went on: "Brothers, if you really love poor Ying, I suggest that in honor of her wedding day—the only holiday of her life, as you put it—we change from these glasses to man-sized bowls." He quickly took another piece of meat.

"Bravo! Let's change," said a smaller boy, whose voice was clearer, sharper. "I have to admit, I was surprised when you brought out these little glasses. I mean, I thought maybe this was intended as a joke. Which would be more like insulting our sister than congratulating her."

Now they were all shouting. "Let's change to bowls! Let's change to bowls!"

Large bowls were brought, and more alcohol flowed. But no one drank; everyone was eating.

"Come on, Cousin Number Three, empty your bowl," urged the big boy called Old Fourth. "You're the one who asked for bowls."

Three looked up, staring at his brother like a hungry wolf. "Empty it I shall," he said. "But don't rush me. In honor of our sister, I'll drink every drop. . . . But let's be fair, Old Fourth. You've had one glass less. Why don't you catch up? Then we can go on together."

Grandfather Liu sat in the middle of the big bed watching everyone drink. Absent-mindedly, he smoked his long-stemmed pipe, happy to see almost the whole family gathered together. Liu wasn't drinking either. He sat in a corner in the shadows, where no one would notice him. For him, the festivities were a source of sadness: they marked the departure of his oldest daughter, who had been a pillar of the household, indispensable to him.

Liang and Tian ate, and had a little to drink.

"Do you want to see the bride?" Tian asked.

"Yes, I'd like that," answered Liang, a little lost in the alcoholic haze.

They went to the east room, which was reserved, as usual on holidays, for the women. There they found Grandmother Liu, Tian's mother, and their guests. The women were talking more than eating. They drank a very sweet red wine.

To Liang's surprise, Ying—dressed in brand-new red clothes, with a bright flower in her hair—sat in the corner in tears. An old neighbor, whom everyone called Great-Aunt, was holding a white handkerchief and, with theatrical gestures, trying to console Ying.

"Now, now, my beauty, don't worry so much," she scolded. "You're getting married, and that is cause for great joy. Of course you're sad to be leaving the home you grew up in. Everyone's sad when they have to move out of their parents' house. But this is still your home, you know, you can come back whenever you want. . . ."

Far from being calmed, Ying seemed more unhappy. She cried louder. The old woman went on, talking with her mouth full. The other women paid no attention.

"Yes, it's sad," Liang heard the woman closest to him say. "I still remember the night before my wedding day. 'Starting tomorrow, daughter,' my mother told me, 'you will be a member of another family. You will have to fend for yourself. You won't be a child anymore, as you are here.' And I burst out crying."

"Yes," said another. "Home is so familiar. You know where everything is; your parents are always there. You may fight with your brothers and sisters, but once you realize that you'll never really belong at home again, that you'll be just a guest when you come back, you feel you can't stand it."

"You're right, sisters," added an older woman. "That's what's so hard about a woman's lot. Before she marries, all she does is work, and everything she earns goes to her brothers. Then, when she goes to her new family, she becomes her in-laws' servant, the servant of relatives she doesn't even know. We never really have a place of our own in this life."

Ying cried louder. Great-Aunt was working hard with her white handkerchief, bringing all her powers of persuasion to bear.

"Let her cry," Grandmother Liu said. "Let her cry all she wants. It's a good sign. She's leaving her childhood behind in this house. Tomorrow she becomes an adult in her in-laws' house. We want her to act right, so they won't say we brought her up badly."

Great-Aunt wiped her own eyes with the handkerchief and nodded approval of Grandmother's reasoning.

"It's true, Big Sister," she said. "Crying is a way of growing up, a way of changing. Take the wife of that boy Young Old. She must be over forty, but she acts just like a child. They say she didn't cry the night before her wedding."

"I can understand my sister Ying," a younger woman said. "She's crying because she's sad. And why is she sad on the eve of such a happy event? After all, she's more fortunate than some of us. At least she knows her future husband, and he seems to be about the best catch around. His family has a good reputation and is well off too. So if Ying is crying, it's because she's so attached to her parents and grandparents. And that's no surprise: anyone, no matter how hard-hearted, would cry at having to leave them."

The women's chatter flowed on, and so did the future bride's tears.

Ying's crying made Liang uncomfortable. Two red peonies were embroidered on her chest, one over each breast, and they shook up and down as she sobbed. She's getting married tomorrow, Liang said to himself, and he pictured the palanquin sent by the husband's family. It would arrive in the morning to take Ying away. Unless they were given an extra tip, the two men who carried it would deliberately jostle poor Ying, already so sad at leaving her home and so worried about meeting her new family.

"A new daughter-in-law is a slave, there's no doubt about that," Grandmother Liu suddenly said.

And Ying, her sweet, tender face wet with tears, would be the slave. Liang imagined her having to wake up at the crack of dawn to light the fire, make breakfast for the whole family, and feed the squealing pigs and the chickens. Then there would be the work in the fields and the household chores. Also, she would have to take care of the grandparents and mind her mother-in-law, and mind her husband too, of course.

The racket the men were making in the other room bothered the women. With a worried air, they speculated about which among their husbands would be the first to get drunk and which the last. They knew what would come next: the difficult return home, the drunken insults they would suffer, the vomit-stained clothes they would have to take off and clean, the revolting smell of alcohol. Still, they were curious about what was going on in the other room. But they dared not go to see. That would bring scorn upon the husband and abuse upon the wife.

Ying stopped crying. She sat quietly on the bench, her eyes puffy. Grandmother Liu looked at Great-Aunt, whose tiny eyes brightened in response. "Now?" she asked mysteriously.

Grandmother nodded, and the old woman moved closer to Ying, bouncing along the bed. She put her hand over her mouth as though about to tell some secret.

Liang heard her say in a peculiar voice: "Listen, my girl. There are things we usually don't mention, but I've been waiting to speak to you about them. One reason you marry is, of course, to raise a family, to have children. That is the most sacred duty of marriage. You'll soon find out that men are a little hard to take at first, but be docile and submissive. The best thing is to get pregnant as soon as possible, and to have a son first."

Ying blushed; even her ears got red. She lowered her eyes and dropped her shoulders.

Great-Aunt shifted closer and kept talking. "Do you understand, my girl? We've all gone through it; it's our common lot. So don't act surprised when the time comes. Don't do anything stupid, or you'll be the laughingstock of the whole region. It hurts the first time, and there will be a little blood. But it's not a real injury, so there's no need to be afraid."

Ying turned redder, pushed the old woman away timidly, and gave a quick glance at the two boys.

"Get out of here!" Great-Aunt shouted at them. "Men have no right to be in our room. You're far too young to hear any of this anyway."

Liang and Tian, confused, immediately left the room. They were delighted, though, that they had been able to eavesdrop on female secrets.

Tian look Liang's hand as they left. "Come and look at something," he said.

In a corner of the courtyard was a narrow space between two walls. Tian lit a lamp made from an empty ink bottle and said to Liang, "This is my place."

Liang peered into a recess barely a foot wide, through which water drained out of the courtyard. A strong putrid smell rose from it.

Tian crouched like a shrimp, his head against his knees, and disappeared.

Liang hesitated.

"Come and see," Tian urged, as though he were about to reveal the world's greatest secret.

Liang crouched down, held his breath, and followed Tian into the drain, where chickens wandered freely.

"There! You see?" Tian asked.

Liang had closed his eyes when he crawled into the space. Now he forced himself to open them and saw two little wheels mounted on small posts and tied together by string.

"What is it?" he asked, slightly disappointed.

Tian searched his friend's eyes for admiration. When he failed to find it, he hesitated before deciding to explain.

"I'll tell you. But you have to promise to keep it a secret."

"I promise."

"This is an electricity plant," Tian began in a solemn tone. "The two wheels are linked. See? When I turn this one, the other one moves at the same time."

Naturally, Liang thought.

"Put your hand here." Tian took Liang's hand and placed it on the second wheel. Then he began to spin the first one very fast.

"Do you feel anything?" he asked.

"No," Liang answered, quickly pulling his hand away from the heat.

"What do you mean?" Tian was annoyed. "Didn't you feel the heat?"

"Yes."

"Well, that's the electricity. You remember when the teacher told us that if you rub two . . . I forget exactly . . . but anyway, the two objects make electricity. See, we can produce it right here. All we have to do is spin this wheel, and the other produces electricity. Then we put in light bulbs, first here in my place, then in your room. We'll be the first in the district to have electricity."

Liang listened, more fascinated by his friend than by the project.

"All we need are a few more power plants," Tian added.

Liang thought for a moment. "What you say is true," he said carefully. "But suppose we wanted to make enough electricity to light the bulbs in your house and mine at the same time. We'd get awfully tired keeping the wheels turning."

Tian mulled over that. "You're right," he admitted. "It would be hard work."

They lay side by side in silence, as motionless as leaves chilled by a frost.

"Wait a minute," Liang exclaimed. "I have an idea. We can put in a motor driven by the electricity, and the motor will keep the wheels turning. That way the whole thing will work by itself."

Tian's eyes shone, and so did Liang's. The two boys lay there in the dung-splattered dark, electrified, dreaming, hatching new plans, new fantasies.

One evening, as they lay in their hiding place dreaming, the boys heard footsteps. Someone stopped at the black door, knocked, and shouted, "Uncle Liu, Uncle Liu."

Liu went to the door.

"Tonight's the night."

"I know. I'll be right there."

Liu said a few words to someone inside the house, then left quickly.

Tian looked meaningfully at Liang.

"What is it?" Liang asked.

Tian blinked. "Do you want to go see?" he asked.

"Why not?"

The boys backed out of the narrow passage, rear ends in the air like chickens. They followed Liu, whose indistinct shadow had not yet left the alley. One behind the other, silent, they walked with mystery in their hearts.

When he left the alley, Liu turned in front of the church and walked faster. The boys did too.

"Do you know where he's going?" Liang asked.

"To Uncle Old Black's," Tian answered confidently.

"Why?"

"I don't know. He goes there a lot. I've followed him a few times, but they always close the door too fast. So I've never been able to find out what they do."

十二

Liu turned right and entered another alley, on the out-skirts of the village.

Tian spoke as they walked. "I was alone the other times, and I was afraid to try to open the door. This time there are two of us, so let's try to see what's going on. All right?"

"Yes," Liang said, gripping his friend's hand.

They waited at the entrance to the alley and saw Liu glance back a few times before going through a door. They heard the sound of a bolt.

Then silence.

"Let's go," Tian said.

But he didn't move. Neither did Liang, who felt as if something heavy in the night was hanging over them, wait-ing to fall on their heads.

"What does this Uncle Old Black look like?" Liang whispered.

"I don't know," Tian muttered. "He never comes out."

"You mean you've never seen him?"

"I did once, when I was little, but I don't remember."

Liang looked at his friend in the darkness, then at the door.

"Well, shall we try?" Tian asked in a faint voice. He clearly hoped the answer would be "No."

Liang did not answer. He looked up at the dark sky, the sparkling stars. Occasional twitters could be heard among the leaves of the nearby trees, but not a soul moved in the deserted street. He thought it must be very late, the first time he had ever been out so late. He could picture his mother's reproachful look at his father, who always took Liang's side when his mother said he couldn't go out.

"Do you want to go home?" Tian asked.

"No!" Liang almost shouted, surprising himself. "Let's go see."

"All right, then," Tian replied.

Liang moved forward, hearing his own footsteps, and Tian's close behind them.

"Does the old man have a dog?"

"Yes," Tian whispered.

A few more steps, taken hand in hand, brought the boys to the courtyard door. It was very old, cracked, and dark. When they saw no sign of a dog, they heaved a sigh of relief.

From behind a low wall topped with dead grass that looked black in the darkness came the faint sound of music.

"Oh! Now I understand!" Tian exclaimed.

"What is it?" Liang asked, getting ready to run.

"It's a mass."

"A what?"

"A mass. I've heard my grandmother hum that tune plenty of times."

"Mass?" Liang repeated the word, not knowing what it meant. He listened to the music, so faint and high he felt he would have to leap into the air to catch it and drag it down to his ears. The only music he had ever heard had been the song of the birds in the morning, the chirping of crickets in the evening, the patter of raindrops on the window at night, and the whistling of the winter wind. He strained to take in this mass, this music, a group of sounds that seemed to flow all together. Some of the sounds were deep, some high; they intertwined and weaved around one another. When one sound leaped forward, the others dashed to catch up. This was brighter than the tinkling of the bell on the goat's neck, more cheerful than the murmur of a brook, more tender than an animal's sigh. Liang was captivated.

The music rose again, and was followed by deep male

voices, like the hum of bees. It sounded like a lot of people.

"Do you want to go in?" asked Tian, who pushed at the door without waiting for Liang's answer.

Liang would have said no had the door not been bolted. "How can we get in?" he asked instead.

"Easy," said Tian, rummaging in his pockets. "Do you have anything thin and hard? A knife, a ruler?"

"I have a penknife."

"Perfect." Tian took Liang's little knife, opened it, slid it between the panels of the door, and tried to lift the bolt.

Liang felt such a weight pressing down on him that he held his breath until Tian was done. As the door opened with a slight creak, they felt a cold draft.

In the courtyard, they saw that the house was actually a barn, its windows lit by candles. Their hearts pounding, they crept to the door. Through its cracks, they saw about twenty men kneeling in front of an old man with a beard. He was dressed in white, his eyes were closed, and he was singing in a faraway voice. Sometimes the others would say something with him and then make a ten in front of their chests with their fingers.

Behind the old man in white was a statue of a man hanging on a big ten, like the one Liang had noticed on the church. The music was coming from an old phonograph.

A strange feeling came over Liang as he watched the mysterious movements of these tired, undernourished men dressed in old clothes, their spines bent from years of toil in rain and sun. Now they bowed even lower, before the old man in white and the statue of the man so cruelly nailed. The candles did not dissipate the gloom that lay over sound and silence. Liang felt something he knew he had felt before—perhaps in a dream, or in the old tales his mother told him when he was small. He felt that part of his mind was mingling with these kneeling men as they made their sign, raised their eyes to the barn's ceiling, and recited words that he could not understand.

The music faded, and the ceremony seemed to be over. But a man got up and turned to face the others.

"It's your father!" Liang said, elbowing his friend.

A flash of the eyes was Tian's only answer.

Liu, at a table beside the old man, began to speak: "Brothers, let us pray that God will save us from this drought and this poverty."

Once again they knelt, and Liu led a new chant.

十三

The steamed corn bread, made with last year's flour and dignified with the name "golden pagoda," was harsh and dry and left a bitter aftertaste. It was served with bland, sticky corn mush that oozed between your teeth. A few pieces of salted vegetables were added as a side dish to generate a bit of saliva, but they always dried up before you could eat much.

Liang chewed mechanically, unable to swallow. He watched his mother and sister, wondering if it tasted different to them. This was how things were when his father was not home. His mother, exhausted by her day's work, made no attempt to cook anything interesting. All they ate were these three traditional dishes.

"Is that all you're going to eat?" Wang asked.

"No. I'm not finished yet." Liang began to chew again, making an exaggerated noise with his lips.

"There's no point pretending," said Wang. "I know you don't like the food, and I'm not blaming you for that—but I think you're wrong. I'm not saying you're spoiled, because no one has ever spoiled you, but you are . . . ungrateful. Do you know what children used to eat before the liberation? Sorghum bread or, worse, millet husks, rotten millet husks. They didn't have any salted vegetables, and a meal with corn was considered a treat. Today, thanks to the Party and Chairman Mao, we have corn to eat. We must remember that two-thirds of the peoples of this world live under rotten capitalism and starve to death."

Any defense would be futile, for a son can hide nothing from his mother. Liang lowered his eyes and felt ashamed. He was ungrateful, he had to admit. If it weren't for the Party and Chairman Mao, he would have starved. He should be happy; he should listen to his parents, who knew what things were like in the old days. He should eat his corn bread and think about how much better it tasted than sorghum or millet husks.

He opened his mouth wide, put in a big piece of golden pagoda and some mush, and began to chew noisily, trying to show enthusiasm.

"*I* don't hate corn," said little Ling.

But I hate you, Liang thought.

Every time his mother criticized him, Ling piped up like that. The truth was, she had expressed her disgust for corn bread many times.

"Of course not," Wang said in a singsong voice. "You're Chairman Mao's good little girl."

Ling took another piece of bread and asked, "Does he know?"

"What?"

"Does he know that I'm his good little girl?"

Wang hesitated. "Of course," she said. "He knows everything. He knows that you always eat your corn and that you never cry when you go to Grandmother Song's while Mama and Papa are working for the Revolution."

"Oh, I'm glad," Ling squealed.

Liang watched in amazement as his sister continued to

eat. How did she swallow so easily, and with that look of delight? Where did she get so much saliva? Maybe her tongue was still too little to taste bitter things.

"I ran into Papa in the street," Ling said.

"Really?" Liang asked. "What was he doing?" He had not seen his father in four days.

"He was with some people."

"You didn't call to him, did you?" This time it was Wang who stopped eating.

"Yes. I called him three times."

"Did he see you?" Liang asked.

"Yes. He waved at me. But I knew he was working and I shouldn't bother him. I let him go off with those people he was with. I even smiled good-bye at him. I'm good, aren't I, Mama?"

Wang stroked Ling's head without answering. Liang was filled with envy. He never had a chance to run into his father, being stuck in school all day. But if he ever did run into him, he would be just as heroic, he would be Chairman Mao's good little boy. In fact, to get that glorious title, he would accept gladly the sacrifice of not seeing his father even for several days.

Liang wiped his mouth. "That's all," he said. "I'm not hungry anymore."

Wang looked at him with piercing eyes. "If you don't want to start your schoolwork right away, why don't you walk your sister to Grandmother Song's."

"Can't I stay home tonight?" Ling asked sadly.

"No. I have too much work to do, and your brother also has a lot of work," Wang said. "You, Ling, are still too little to work. But, if you go to Grandmother Song's and let us do our work, you, too, will be helping the Revolution."

"But I won't make any noise if you let me stay." She

had stopped eating and was drawing circles on the table with her dirty little fingers.

Since Liang felt like going out, he offered her some encouragement: "Don't you want to be Chairman Mao's good little girl now?"

"Yes . . . I do," she murmured.

"Then come with me, if you're brave enough."

Ling sat, pouting. "I'll go if you promise you won't be late coming to get me," she finally said.

"Of course," Wang said, getting up from the table.

Ling reluctantly stood up and gave Liang her hand.

He felt its small warmth in his palm and squeezed a little, expecting his sister to squeeze back. But her hand lay motionless in his, like a piece of cotton. He noticed that she was moving very slowly, as she always did when she had to leave the house, whereas he liked to fly out into the street as fast as possible. The girl was hopeless, he thought. Too attached to the house, to her parents. She had no future at all.

"Do you want to ride on my back, Ling?" he asked.

"Well . . . all right."

He crouched down so she could get on, then started walking fast.

"Tell Mama not to forget to come and get me before nine," Ling said in his ear.

"Yes," Liang answered. "But why don't you want to go to Grandmother Song's?"

Ling said nothing.

"Come on, tell me."

"You won't tell Mama if I tell you?"

"No."

"I'm afraid."

"Of what?"

"Of Grandmother Song."

"Why?"

"She tells me bad stories when I cry."

"Why do you cry? That's not nice."

"Yes, but . . . oh, I don't know."

"Well, don't do it anymore."

"I won't."

When they reached the alley where Grandmother Song lived, Liang put his sister down. "Go on," he said. "You know which door it is."

"Aren't you coming with me?"

"What for? I'm in a hurry." He turned and left her without a glance back.

Liang ran to the church and stopped at the big gate of Party headquarters. It was not locked yet, but he saw no one in the courtyard. After hesitating for a moment, he climbed the three stone steps and went to the door under the archway.

"What do you want?" a harsh voice asked, as a window opened in the wall. Liang saw an old man's badly shaved face regarding him.

"I'm looking for my father," Liang said quickly.

"Who's your father?"

"Li Xian Yang."

"Prefect Li?" The old man's eyes brightened, and his voice softened.

"You're Li Liang, aren't you? You can go and look for your father if you want, but I don't think he's here. He's always out."

"He's not in his office?" Liang asked, his throat tight.

"You're welcome to go and see. His office is down there, at the end of the courtyard, on the left."

Reassured by the caretaker's kindness, Liang went toward his father's door. Should he call out "Papa" before going in? Would his father be angry at the interruption? For a moment, Liang almost hoped that the caretaker was right, that his father was out. He stood looking at the door, listening. It was a new door, but already cracked by the dry climate, like so many doors in the village. He peered through a crack. All he could see were the four legs of a table. He looked for his father's two legs, but there was no sign of them.

I guess he's not in, Liang said to himself. Feeling bolder, he pushed the door. At first it made a noise as if it would give way. But it didn't, though he pushed again. The door wouldn't open. Liang squatted on the steps, his back against the door, pleased that this was Li's door at his back, solid and generous, like his father's chest. Then he sat down on the ground and stretched out his legs.

As he looked around the courtyard, he realized that he was sitting directly opposite the church, whose side door stared at him suspiciously, like a vertical eye. Shuddering, he remembered Song's words. "We've turned that building, where foreigners tried to poison our people with religion, into the headquarters of the Party Committee."

The courtyard was deserted by this time of the evening; the commune officials had gone home. And of course there was no one in the church, once holy, now a place forbidden to everyone but him, the prefect's only son.

He got up and headed for the church. All the muscles of his body tensed when the side door swung open. He had expected it to be very heavy, to creak loudly. But it opened almost by itself.

He walked fearfully, but filled with curiosity, into the huge, pitch-dark building. The first thing he noticed was the sharp, penetrating smell of mildew. Holding his breath, he waited for his eyes to get used to the darkness. The building was very tall and almost empty—just a few long tables in the middle, with a dozen benches scattered around. The ceiling was made of intersecting arches that rested on large columns. In front was a platform. A bell hung high above, its cord dangling to the floor. He touched the cord and heard a faint noise. The only other sound was the echo of his footsteps, which made him shiver.

Song's words rang in his ears, and suddenly he felt dizzy. He looked up at the high platform, at the even higher bell.

"Papa can't dig wells at night, Mama. It's too dark," the little girl said suddenly. Liang, lying in bed beside her, was thinking about the church.

"This is the third time I've had to tell you to go to sleep," an irritated Wang answered, looking up from the papers she was correcting. "Anyway, your father does other things besides digging wells."

"Tell me what he's doing so late at night, and I'll go to sleep."

"Promise?"

"I promise."

"Very well. There's a Party meeting."

"No. The Party meeting was last night."

"Well, there's another one tonight. Go to sleep now!"

"There are too many Party meetings." Ling sighed, turned her back to Liang, and closed her eyes.

Liang also turned around. His schoolwork had made him sleepy. But his sister was right: there were far too many Party meetings. He remembered something Grandfather Liu had said: "The Nationalist Party has a lot of taxes; the Communist Party has a lot of meetings." What were taxes? He closed his eyes and listened to the scratching of his mother's pen. It was fun to try to guess which of her comments were good and which were critical. A loud scratch that tailed off softly and smoothly meant a good grade; two loud quick scratches meant the pupil had made a

mistake. Liang could also hear the paper rustle when she turned a page or went on to a different paper. From that, he could figure out how many good students and how many bad students there were in his mother's class.

He listened for a long time, but finally tired of it. He opened his eyes and looked at the wall right in front of his nose. Close up, the many marks and blotches on it looked enormous. He tried to pick out shapes: a cotton cloud, the face of the Ape King, the head of the pig Grandfather Liu had killed, the dirty hair of the girl whose head blocked his view of the blackboard, a broken church ten, a tree uprooted by the wind whose sound was the scratching of Wang's pen.

His mother was now crossing things out more vigorously. Many mistakes.

Outside, there was no sound at all, not even the chirp of a cricket. If only he could hear footsteps through the nervous scratching of Wang's pen, just as he had the other night: barely noticeable at first, but then getting louder and louder, the sound of his father's shoes on the gravel, then the heavier tread on the two concrete steps at the door.

There had been no footsteps so far tonight. But they would come. By the time he heard them, his father would be very close, so there was no point in straining to hear. But if Liang had sharp ears, so sharp that he could hear when his father left the meeting in the church, then he could follow him as he walked past the alley where the Lius lived. Li knew that his son had a friend there, so he would think about Liang when he passed that house. Liang imagined the rest of the walk home, picturing the pond with dirty water, where you had to hold your breath and walk fast to get away from the smell, then the school gate and the courtyard. After the gate, Liang knew, there were twenty-seven more steps for his father.

He opened his eyes and listened, but heard only the scratching of the pen.

He closed his eyes again to wait. Maybe he had been too quick when he pictured his father's walk home. And his father would be thinking not only about Liang. There would be other things on his mind: the meeting, the number of wells they had dug. He must be coming past the alley now, turning right along the pond.

Liang almost fell asleep despite himself. He turned over and looked at his sister.

"Aren't you asleep yet?" Wang asked.

"No," said Liang, ashamed.

"It's after eleven. If you don't go to sleep, you won't be able to get up tomorrow."

"I'll go to sleep now. . . . But . . ."

"But what?"

"Did you wait for your father to come home at night when you were little?"

"No," Wang said, after a pause.

"Why not?"

"My father died before I was born," Wang said.

Then she told him the story.

"My father—your grandfather—was a hero of the Eighth Route Army. He had just finished his university studies when the war against the Japanese broke out. He decided to join the Communist Party and go fight the Japanese invaders. Your grandmother was very young, but already pregnant, when he left. Since he was one of the few intellectuals in the Party, he quickly rose in rank and was given more and more responsibility.

"Here's a photograph of him," she said, opening a drawer. Liang got up, took the photograph, and saw a man in an old uniform with braid on the shoulders and a flat cap. Though the picture had yellowed with age, he could still see courage and heroism in the face of that officer, his own grandfather.

"He died in combat. . . . The picture is yours if you want it." She put it in a notebook in the back of the drawer.

"Your grandfather was a hero, Liang. I'm his only daughter, and you're my only son. There's an old saying: 'The sons continue what the fathers have begun.' Your grandfather fought the invader, and his comrades founded a new society, which you, with the rest of your generation, must build and lead to Communism. That's why you have to listen to your parents, because we're the revolutionary cadres, and you have to study hard so that someday . . ."

"What's Communism?"

Wang thought for a moment. "Communism is a society in which there is no exploitation, no poverty, no famine, and where everyone is free."

"And what my father is doing now, it's building Communism?"

"He is the Party leader for this district. Everything he does is for the Party."

Liang asked no more questions. He would no longer lie awake waiting for his father to come home. If Li was late, it was because he had so much to do to bring about this paradise, this happiness. Liang had to let him do his work, had to stop lying awake waiting for the sound of his footsteps.

The sun, dipping into the foaming multi-colored water, splattered the sky with red and black clouds. Liang squinted, leaving the tiniest slit for the dazzling light. He tried to measure the sun's speed, but the sun seemed to realize what he was trying to do and it held still too. I'll get you, Liang thought. But though he could not catch the sun moving, it drew closer and closer to the clouds, to crush them. Liang gave up. He hurled a clump of earth at the sun, lay down on the ground, and began to daydream.

"This is the greatest, most wonderful epoch in history. A red epoch with many revolutionary heroes. To the list of our heroes—Lei Feng, Zhang Jie, Hu Yang Hai, Dong Cun Rui, Huan Ji Gong—we must now add Jiao Yu Lu, prefect of a district in the province of Henan, who has given his life in the bitter struggle against the spread of the desert. He died for the people and for Communism. The Central Committee calls upon all revolutionary people to follow his example, to sing his praises, and hail his heroic exploits far and wide."

A cloud turned crimson, flashed its white and yellow chest, and made ready to absorb the sun, which now seemed weary. Other clouds rose up to show their joy at having escaped annihilation, or perhaps they were jealous at not having received that glorious light.

"Liang, he sounds a lot like your father."

Tian had whispered this in his ear and poked him in the ribs right in the middle of political activities class, which made Liang feel a strange mixture of pride and regret. True, Liang's father was a prefect too, and he too was waging a bitter struggle against drought for the good of the people and the Party. But Li was not the one the principal had been holding up as an example. Because Li was still alive. . . .

Liang shivered. The sun had dropped into the burning water, leaving the land in desolate shadow. He stretched his arms and legs.

He knew that to be a hero of the Revolution, to earn the Party's praise, was the best thing in life. But there was one problem. He thought of the heroes mentioned, whose names he knew by heart. Lei Feng, a soldier of the People's Liberation Army, had died in a truck he was driving for the army. Zhang Jie, also a soldier, had thrown himself on a land mine to save the lives of three peasants. Hu Yang Hai had jumped under the wheels of a cannon being pulled by a runaway horse, thus saving two children who would have been crushed. Dong Cun Rui had held up the roof of a tunnel under an enemy fortification with his bare hands. Huan Ji Gong had plugged the hole of an enemy pillbox with his chest. All these heroes were dead. In fact, they were heroes because they were dead. If you didn't die, you couldn't be a hero.

"Before he left the hospital, Comrade Jiao Yu Lu learned that he had cancer of the liver. He was very tired and in constant pain. But he thought only of his work, and of the people of his district. He kept his disease a secret and wedged a stick between his body and the desk to ease his pain as he worked. It was only after his death that the stick was noticed."

When the principal had said this, Liang couldn't help thinking of his father's desk. He'd remembered seeing the four legs through the crack in the door. Was there a stick like that in the desk? Maybe his father was sick too, keeping his disease a secret and continuing his work. You found out about acts of heroism only after the hero's death. Liang tried to imagine what they might find in his father's desk after he died.

Then he felt a twinge. He loved his father too much to imagine him dead. But then that thought made him feel guilty, because he knew you were not supposed to be afraid to die for the Revolution. Otherwise you could never be a hero. Maybe death wasn't so terrible. He decided he would rather his father died for the Revolution. Liang would die for it too if he had to.

"To fear death is to be like a pig," it was said. Liang thought about the pig at Tian's, the loud squeals, and he remembered the strange sensation he'd felt when the knife was twisted in the blood.

But now suddenly the sun reappeared between two clouds and turned as crimson as Ying's wedding clothes. Liang rubbed his eyes and moved away from Tian, who had been busily cutting grass.

Tian stopped work. "Look at this," he said.

Liang saw that his friend was holding the thin stalk of a plant with little white berries.

"What is it?"

"It's called the star plant."

Liang took it and turned it in his fingers.

"Pretty. What's it for?"

"Don't you know?" Tian smiled. "You can find your way with the star plant. When the sky is cloudy, you can't tell directions. So you pick a star plant and hold it in your mouth, between your teeth. Then, if you close your eyes, you can see the stars."

"You mean you can see stars in the daytime with this?"

"Sure. Try it and see," said Tian, pretending to work, but inching closer.

Liang, after some hesitation, closed his eyes and put the plant between his teeth. All he saw were red, black, and blue spots swarming around under his eyelids. He was about to tell his friend that it wasn't true, when Tian tugged sharply at the stem. Bunches of tiny white berries came off in Liang's mouth.

"You dog!" Liang screamed, spitting frantically. The more he tried to spit them out, the deeper the hairy rough berries got into his throat.

Tian staggered with laughter. Liang tried to grab him, but Tian ran away. Soon they were playing tag in the middle of the field. Then they wrestled for a while, demolishing furrows and crushing sorghum plants.

The clouds took on twisted shapes in the last glimmers of the setting sun, and the wind came up. The boys fell to the ground, out of breath, sweat and dust making brownish mud on their bodies. They lay like two muddy eels, silently staring up at the growing menace of the clouds. Finally Tian stood up.

"If I don't come home with a full basket, my father will send me to bed without supper."

Liang lay there, feeling good pressed against the soil, which was not too hard and not too soft. It was as though he were afloat on a calm sea. Laziness spread over him. He closed his eyes again and breathed deeply, smelling the sweetness of sorghum mixed with the bitter taste of yellow dust.

He turned over to watch Tian work. Suddenly he felt guilty that he was not helping his friend, who would have to go to bed without supper if he didn't fill his basket. No matter how boring the work was, he ought to help Tian. If he couldn't do this, how would he ever find the strength to perform the heroic deeds he dreamed of?

Liang was about to get up to help when he heard something behind him. It sounded like an animal's cry from far away, carried by the wind. It grew louder.

"What's that?" he asked.

Tian, absorbed in his work, which always got harder when the sun went down, did not answer.

"Don't you hear that noise?"

"What noise?" Tian asked. He listened, then shook his head.

"That loud noise . . . Can't you hear it? Like a mooing." He felt anxious.

Tian went back to work. "You must be hearing the cry of the Wen Meng," he said.

"What's the Wen Meng?"

"I can't tell you. I've never seen it."

"Listen, it must be coming from some huge animal, bigger than a cow," Liang almost shouted. "How can you not have seen it?"

"No one here has ever seen it," Tian replied. He seemed uneasy, but not surprised.

"It's strange," Liang murmured.

He stood still, alert, mouth open, arms spread wide. He strained to figure out what kind of cry it could be. A powerful yet faint mooing, more solemn than a ship's siren, sharper than the north wind's whistle, vaster than the ocean's waves, deeper than rolling thunder. It was like a symphony of the mountains and the sea, like the agonized howl of dark clouds crushed by the setting sun, like songs of dusk when the world was set ablaze, like the crack the sky made when it struck the ground at the horizon.

Liang tensed, feeling both terror and pleasure as he let himself be pierced by the cry. He could not tell where it came from. It seemed to come from everywhere, from above and below, from the four corners of the earth and the eight points of the universe. Then suddenly the sound was gone.

"Tian," he asked his friend, upset, "do you still hear it?"

Tian listened. "Yes," he said, "just like before."

"I can't hear it anymore."

"That's because you're listening too hard," Tian explained without stopping his work. "That's the way it is. When you try too hard to hear it, it disappears."

Liang was intrigued.

Tian had cut quite a lot of grass, but it was getting dark. "Let's go home," he said.

"Do you have enough to fill the basket?"

"Let's see."

Liang held the basket, and Tian began to load it, fluffing up the grass to increase the volume. There still wasn't enough to fill the basket.

"What do we do now?" Liang asked. "I should have helped you instead of listening to that crazy sound."

"It's all right. I have an idea."

He took out a pruning knife, cut three stalks of sorghum, and put them at the bottom of the basket. Now the grass almost reached the top.

"Will your father let you eat supper?"

Tian thought about it. "Well, the basket's not full, but it's dark, so he won't be able to see too well. And I'll think of some story to tell him, so he won't look much."

"You could tell about that sound we heard," Liang suggested as they walked.

"No. That's nothing new."

High among the gray clouds, a last glimmer of daylight was barely visible; night had already fallen on the earth below, and mist was spreading through the fields. The boys walked faster along the road that snaked toward the village. As they got near, they could smell that mixture of smoke and corn that always makes children feel especially hungry at that hour. They passed corn, then millet, and finally a melon field. The scent of the ripe fruit wafted toward them.

"The melons must be sweet," Liang said, his mouth watering.

"Yes," said Tian. "The worse the weather is for plants, the better the melons taste."

They slowed down, stopped.

"Look at the size of that one!"

"That one over there is even bigger!"

Their eyes met. They looked around carefully, but saw no one in the fields. The night would protect them.

Tian put the basket down. "Let's rest awhile," he said.

Before he had even finished speaking, Liang dashed into the field and picked the largest melon. Tian took another. They sat down at the edge of the field and started eating.

"Stop!" a voice yelled from behind them. They turned and saw a young man emerge from the millet field. He must have hidden there when he saw them coming.

"I've been waiting for you," the man said, grabbing each boy by the arm. "Let's go. I'm taking you to the Commune Committee."

The boys hung their heads and froze.

"Come on, let's go! You have the nerve to steal melons, so you should have the nerve to face the Committee." When he saw that the boys didn't want to move, he added: "There's an old saying that a brave man is always brave enough to own up when he's done wrong. So show a little courage and come with me. Or they'll accuse me of not doing my job."

Liang pictured himself standing before a Committee official, eyes lowered, listening to a lecture. If they took him before Aunt Song, it might be less harsh, but his father would find out. The principal would give a long speech about Liang's theft, exposing the wickedness of the act and making an example of him before the other pupils, who would laugh scornfully. Liang pictured his mother's grief. He remembered Grandmother Liu's words: "Only to a general's family can a general be born." His dreams of becoming a hero, a worthy successor to his father and grandfather, would be ruined.

Tian began to cry. He was probably thinking that his father would send him to bed without supper.

"Uncle," Liang said, casting an imploring look at the melon guard, "please forgive us this one time. We swear we'll never do it again."

"Too late," the guard said.

Tian cried louder, and Liang had to struggle to hold back the sobs in his own throat. "Please forgive us, Uncle," he said. "We were just so hungry that we couldn't help it. Please let us go home. We'll be grateful to you for the rest of our lives."

Liang had no idea where such fine words had come from.

The melon guard thought about it. He looked around. "All right," he said. "I'll let you off this time, but you have to do something for me."

"Anything, Uncle, if only you don't tell the Committee."

"Come with me, then," the guard ordered.

Tian hoisted the basket to his shoulder, and they followed the guard.

"It's not very far," he said. They went into the millet field. "First of all," the guard said, "if you're so hungry, go ahead and eat the melons you picked."

Tian and Liang looked at each other, not wanting to obey.

"Eat them, I said!" the guard ordered in a harsher tone.

The boys ate the melons as though performing a chore.

"Good. Now let's get to work."

He took off his trousers, lay down on his back, and said, "Pump it!"

The boys watched in horror as he spread his legs. His penis, rising out of a thick clump of black hair, swelled and stood up.

They felt they would die of shame. Heads hanging, they dared not look at each other or at the guard.

"Do it, or I'll tell the Committee," the guard snapped.

Tian burst into tears again. Liang felt like doing the same, but found he couldn't. He stood still, not knowing what to do.

"Well, what's it going to be?" the guard growled.

Liang's head was spinning. He realized that if he wanted to keep his hopes of revolutionary heroism alive, if he wanted to avoid having to face his mother, if he wanted to be allowed to go out after school, he had better obey.

"I'm tired of waiting," the guard said, moving as if to get up.

"I'll do it," Liang murmured.

"Hurry up, then."

Not daring to hesitate any longer, he knelt by the guard, took the big penis in his child's hand, and began to pump it. Disgust shuddered from his fingertips, went up his arm, coursed through his body, and gripped his throat. His hand seemed to blaze like a torch. But he closed his eyes, gritted his teeth, and continued the mechanical movement.

The guard began to moan.

Liang was walking quickly, joy in his heart. "Not so fast," Tian complained. He was having trouble keeping up.

"I always walk like this," Liang protested, but he slowed down. The truth was, he never walked this fast: he was practically running. But he didn't want to admit that to his friend. "It's because you're going to see your father," Tian would have said. Liang did not like people to be able to guess what he was thinking. And that included his mother.

"Mama, can I take a walk in the fields before supper?" he had asked her after school.

"What for?"

"I want to see the wells."

"The wells your father's digging?"

"Yes. The ones closest to the village," he said, uncomfortable. "They told us in class today that the first wells are already working, so Tian and I thought we would go see them."

"If you run into your father, ask him to come home for supper tonight."

"Yes, Mama."

Liang began to speed up again, which made Tian jog three steps for every two he walked. They could see the work site in the distance, marked by a swarm of red flags. Liang wondered what he would have lost by telling the truth. Suppose he had said to his mother, "I want to go to the fields to see Papa." Suppose he had admitted to Tian, "Yes, I'm walking fast because I'm going to see my father." Would his mother have said

no? Would his friend have made fun of him? Just the opposite: his mother would have given him permission, and Tian would have approved, because Tian too was going to see his father, who was working alongside Li.

"Look at the water!" Tian cried.

There at their feet was a thin, murky trickle, splitting up like snakes slithering through the clumps of dry earth and the tenuous roots of the plants. Liang could almost hear the earth absorbing it. He could feel the coolness in the field and in his throat as he swallowed his own saliva, mimicking the sucking sound the soil was making.

"Let's follow this little stream and see where it's coming from," Tian suggested, taking off his shoes and walking in the muddy water.

They could hear the voices of the workers. Tian went into a small pond, cupped his hands, and began to drink.

"It tastes so fresh," he said. "Don't you want to try it?"

Liang seemed not to hear his friend. He put his hand over his eyebrows and looked at the group of people in the distance. The dust distorted their silhouettes, making them look like magic shadows lurching and limbless. Suddenly he stopped, stared at one silhouette that moved among the others. It was Li, his father. Liang recognized him by his thin, bowed legs, by his arms, and most of all by the self-confident way he handled his shovel. That had to be his father, the leader of the others.

"I want to go take a look over there," said Liang.

"Me too," said Tian, getting out of the water. "I want to look for my father."

Liang ran toward the workers, his eyes fixed on that one silhouette, trying to ignore the pounding of blood in his ears. Li stopped work when he saw the boys coming.

"Hey, Liang, it's your father!" Tian shouted, nudging

his friend's shoulder as Liang pulled up wordlessly in front of Li.

Everybody had stopped working, and Liang felt slightly shamefaced as the peasants stared stonily at him. His mouth moved, but no sound came out. So he simply smiled.

Li smiled too, then went back to work. "For a minute, I thought something was wrong," he said.

"No," Liang said, taking a step toward his father. "Everything's fine."

"Good," said Li. "In that case, come and see what we're doing. You too, Tian. Your father's here."

The boys skipped up to the well. Liu was digging down below, where the crew had started work again, chattering loudly.

"Papa, it's me," Tian called, leaning over the hole.

"Yes, I see you," Liu called back, his voice loud. "Did you cut a basket of grass?"

"No," Tian answered, disconcerted. "I just came to see you, Papa."

"That's nice, but why didn't you bring food?"

"Food?"

"Because you act as if you were visiting a sick man. And when you visit the sick, you're supposed to bring food. That's the custom."

"What do you mean? Are you sick? Mama didn't give me any food, and she doesn't even know that . . ."

Everyone burst out laughing before Tian could finish his sentence. "Hey, Tian," someone called, "go get your father some ginger. That should fix him up."

Someone else added: "Your mother's bored and sent you to bring your father home?"

More laughter. Liang laughed too, but Tian turned red.

"Insult them back!" Liu murmured.

"Fuck all your mothers!" Tian shouted as loud as he could.

"Watch your language!" Li warned with a smile. He called down to Liu, "Why don't you come up and have a cigarette?"

Liu dug a few more shovelfuls and told the crew to take a rest. When he had sat down beside Li on a pile of freshly dug earth, the men lit cigarettes and began to talk.

Liang sat next to his father, feeling very happy. He watched his father's lips pinch the cigarette as he inhaled. Smoke trickled out when they opened. Liang pretended he was smoking too. He closed his lips when his father inhaled again, then opened them when the smoke came out.

"In ten days we'll have at least forty wells working," Li said.

"Which will mean a hundred acres saved," Liu answered.

"If there's water for irrigation, this land can be very fertile." Li dropped his cigarette on the ground, spat on the butt, and rubbed his chin, looking into the distance.

Liu rolled another cigarette and spoke more personally: "You may not know this yet, Prefect Li, but these fields need more than wells to yield a good harvest."

"What do you mean?"

"We have an unusual climate here. It's always very dry until late August, but after that, when the rainy season comes, it floods."

"Every year?"

"Almost."

Li fell silent. He took a deep breath, as though he were still smoking, then closed his mouth and let the air whistle through his nose. Liang tried to copy his father's gestures.

"How far is it from here?" Li asked, standing and staring to the north.

"To the Dry River, you mean?"

"Yes."

"About five kilometers."

Li thought for a while. "Today's the twelfth of July," he said. "So we have about a month. It should be possible to dig an irrigation ditch to the river by then, if we put half our people on it."

"If we get a ditch dug before the rains come, a good harvest would be guaranteed," said Liu, dragging heavily on his cigarette.

Li stared silently toward the Dry River, whose levee looked like a yellow ribbon in the light of the setting sun. He smacked his fist on his thigh. "We can do it!" he said.

Liu stood up. He was still smoking, but he no longer seemed calm. "Prefect Li," he said, "there's one thing you shouldn't overlook."

"What's that?"

"A ditch nine feet wide with levees on either side will sacrifice a strip of good land at least six meters wide all the way to the river. A lot of plants could grow in that soil. It's asking a lot."

"Yes, you're right. But otherwise we'll lose everything. The peasants are smart enough to understand that."

"Not necessarily. If by some chance there's no flood this year . . ." Liu began, but he did not finish the thought. Li was no longer listening. Liang heard Liu, though, and repeated to himself: Not necessarily.

"It's getting dark," his father said to Liu. "Tell the men to go home and eat. Then go find Song and tell her to get everyone together for a Committee meeting tonight. I'll convince them."

Liu took his son's hand, and they left.

"Let's go," Li said to Liang. He slung his shovel over his shoulder and tapped Liang lightly on the head with his other hand. They headed for the village.

Li walked very fast, as though he were trying to outrun the night. As Liang hurried to stay close, his father's hand, swaying to the rhythm of his gait, brushed his shoulder. Liang looked at that hand and at its fingers stained yellow by cigarette smoke and hardened by work in the fields. He opened his own hand and felt a sad longing in his fingertips. When he was small, he had always held his father's middle finger when they walked. It had seemed so big and strong, though not as rough as it was now. Liang once needed his whole hand to grasp it. That finger had belonged to him, he felt. Not the other fingers; they were either too short or too thin. The middle finger, the biggest one on the left hand, was Liang's, for him to tug on. He remembered when, on a night they had walked to the movies, his father had accidentally held out his index finger. It felt all wrong when Liang took hold of it, and he had to send a thousand signals before his father realized that it was not the right finger. Only when his father changed fingers did their walk feel right again. Another time—it was the day his father took him to school for the first time—Liang felt that his father's big finger had become too thin, that he could no longer squeeze it as tightly in his whole hand. So he had grasped two fingers, the middle and the fourth. But it must not have felt right to his father. He withdrew one and then the other, and their walk lacked its usual harmony.

Maybe that was the day his father stopped holding out his finger, and, instead, started tapping him lightly on the head and saying, "Let's go," just as he had tonight.

Despite the gathering dusk, Liang kept watching his

father's left hand, moving his head to follow it as it swung back and forth. How would his father react if Liang were to reach out for it? What would he do? Offer him the middle finger? Impossible. Liang's hand was much too big for that now. Two fingers? No. Not since his father pulled them away going to school that day. His whole hand? But that would be as if they were only friends, or brothers.

Liang felt a pang as he realized that he would never again be able to hold his father's finger as they walked. That bond between them was gone.

Do you think you'll be able to dig the ditch, Papa? Do you think we'll have a good harvest?

Liang wanted to ask his father these and other questions, but as he watched his father, who walked with his head high, his shoulders slightly hunched, too tall for Liang to see his expression, he knew what the answers would be. His father was a prefect, the leader of the Party Committee, and to such a man such questions would be stupid.

Liang smiled in the darkness.

十
七

The rainy season started after school one day, as Tian and Liang were lying in the filthy space of their electricity laboratory. The failure of countless experiments had sapped their interest, if not their hope, in the two little wheels rigged together with string. The boys had turned to other projects. They had knocked fruit out of the jujube tree with a long bamboo pole, tied a muzzle on the pig and pretended he was a horse, watched a hen laying eggs, made clay disks out of mud and urine, and tried to sleep in a tree. Now they were looking for something new.

"What's the most important thing you can buy with two fen?" Tian asked.

"Let me think," Liang mumbled. What could you get with two fen that was important? Not a couple of pieces of candy—that's what he usually spent two fen on—because candy disappeared the second you ate it. A piece of iron? That would last forever, but you couldn't do much with it. "You can't buy *anything* with two fen," he finally said.

"You can so."

"What?"

"With two fen, I could buy a box of matches and burn the village down. That would be important, wouldn't it?"

No doubt about it, one box of matches could burn the whole village down. Such a fire would be even bigger in the town. Liang looked at Tian with admiration, proud that he had such an intelligent friend.

He was about to speak when they heard a violent clap of thunder. Then louder and louder thunder, until there was a gigantic long rumble.

"Rain!" Tian shouted. "Let's go out!"

The sky had become a roiling sea that throbbed with thunder and was ripped by many-headed dragons spitting fire. A savage wind tore at their shirts.

Rain began to fall in drops the size of little walnuts. Liang was about to suggest that they go inside, but his friend lifted his arms to the sky, shouting, "It's raining, it's raining!" He took Liang by the hand, and they ran out of the courtyard.

They were dazzled by lightning that cracked right above their heads.

"Where are you going?" Liang asked, but the wind, far stronger than his voice, whipped the words away. Tian heard nothing, or pretended to hear nothing. He ran like a demon, dragging Liang along.

They left the alley and entered the bigger street, where all was in confusion. Dogs barked, cats leaped, hens took flight. Old women, their feet bound and their hair undone, dashed out into the street to catch chickens and children. Grownups wearing hats were hurrying home from the fields, shovels on their shoulders. Only the children seemed delighted, their souls rising from hidden depths as they gathered in the rain or under gates. Boys screamed crude songs at the top of their lungs:

> *Rain falls down.*
> *It bubbles on the ground.*
> *Only assholes wear hats.*

The girls sang a more proper song:

Great Lord of Heaven, give us rain.
After the wheat harvest,
We'll invite You to the feast.

The rain did fall heavily, and people wearing straw hats had to take them off.

Tian howled louder than all the other children. Liang, as soon as he recovered from his astonishment, joined in.

The wind gradually died down, but the rain kept falling in a torrent, its deafening sound drowning out the children's chants. Liang and Tian were exhausted from all the shouting. They looked at each other, wondering how to take advantage of such a rare and precious downpour. Tian took his friend by the arm and said, "We'll go out to the fields!"

"In the rain?"

"Why not?"

Liang looked at Tian, trying to figure out why his normally level-headed friend was so excited today. Yet what better thing was there to do during a great upheaval in the sky than to go into the fields in the teeth of the rain and wind and greet the plants, watch the birds fly through heavy clouds, and follow the water as it flowed in streams that gurgled louder and louder?

Tian took off his clothes and shoes, bundled them up under his arm, and ran naked down the street.

Liang did the same, thrilled by the peril and joy of the adventure.

"Faster!"

They bolted out of the village like two fleeing rabbits.

Soon they were in the dark fields. The sky was low, and the rain was thick. They could see only about a yard in front of them.

Holding hands to keep from falling, they dashed wildly

on. It was as if they were running through a big cloud from which they could see neither sky nor earth; all sense of direction was gone. Liang felt nothing but the beating of the rain on his skin. Something inside him drove him forward faster and faster. Without realizing it, he let go of Tian's hand.

"Where are you going?" Tian asked, sounding worried.

"Farther."

Liang said no more. He ran on through the water and mud, trying to purge the burning warmth from his body, to feel the vibration that throbbed in harmony with the sky's torrent. Snatches of images passed before him, things that had been dim in his memory but now were clear: the donkey's hairless rump trudging up the slope; the cloth peddler singing his endless refrain; Tian's sister weeping on the eve of her wedding; the enormous, angry penis of the guard in the melon field; his father's rough middle finger. And many other pictures whipped by before Liang could grasp them.

Suddenly he stepped into emptiness and tumbled into a puddle. He had no strength to get up.

It was quite a while before Tian reached him. When he did, he asked sharply: "Are you crying?"

Liang did not answer, afraid that he might really burst into tears.

"You go too fast." Tian crouched down. The rain was so heavy, they had to lower their heads to breathe.

"Look! We're near the kiln. That's where my grandfather works. Let's go see him."

They ran a little farther and came to the village kiln. As tall as a two-story house, it was made of hard-packed earth. There were no beams or bricks, because they could not withstand the heat of the fire. A low building beside the big kiln served as the workshop. The boys found Grand-father Liu, the pottery master, inside. To their astonish-ment, he was kneeling amid the pottery, hands joined across his chest, forehead bent to the ground. Two apprentices stood motionless beside him, their heads bowed. They were all murmuring indistinct words in a singsong way.

Tian signaled Liang not to make a sound. Having no idea what was going on, Liang listened to the murmuring, which seemed part of the symphony of the storm. He was fascinated by the objects around the workshop: basins with decorated edges, stacked one inside the other, carved bowls, statues of Buddha in different poses, clay whistles shaped like animals. Lumps of dull clay waited their turn in the kiln, where they would be turned into beautiful, shining things.

Grandfather Liu and his apprentices finished their cer-emony and noticed the two boys. The old man scratched his head. "It's very strange," he said somewhat admiringly. "You always seem to show up here whenever it rains. And today you've brought our future prefect with you."

Tian smiled at his grandfather and mimicked his solemn tone: "It's very strange. You always seem to kneel down and start mumbling whenever it rains."

The old man smiled back, but then he looked worriedly at the sky through the torrent that streamed down the windowpane.

"What were you doing, Grandfather?" Liang asked.

The old man shook his head. "Trying to stop the kiln from collapsing, my boy," he muttered through his mus-tache.

Liang did not understand how what they were doing could possibly protect the kiln. But the kiln was certainly in danger.

"It is as old as I am," Grandfather Liu explained patiently, "and that is very old for an oven. It has survived many storms, as I have. All the others built around that time collapsed long ago. This one has fired countless pieces of pottery, has made money for us. Who knows how many of us would have starved to death without it?"

The old man stared silently at the kiln. Then he went on: "Every time it rains, I can hear cracks opening in its body, and in mine too. So I pray for the kiln, pray that it might last a few more years. For myself I don't pray. I've always felt that I would die when it died. . . ."

Liang was disturbed, but Tian seemed not to be paying much attention.

"Are there any pots in it?" he asked.

"Oh yes. It's full," an apprentice answered.

The sky seemed to be getting brighter.

"The rain is going to stop," said Tian, playing the expert.

"I wouldn't be so sure of that," his grandfather answered. "As the old proverb says, 'A single clearing of the sky, ten feet of rain on the earth.' "

An extraordinary thing happened then. Beneath the drumming of the rain, Liang thought he heard that same loud, deep noise he had heard in the fields. "Grandfather," he asked the old man without thinking, "do you know what the Wen Meng is?"

The old man gasped, his eyes wide. Then he regained his composure and gave Liang a stern look. "You must not speak of such a thing at a time like this. It's too dangerous."

Liang was not sure what he felt—curiosity or remorse. "But why, Grandfather? The other day I heard the noise in the fields, and Tian told me it was the Wen Meng. I just wanted to know whether you'd ever seen it."

"Please, not now!" the old man said abruptly, gesturing

at the sky, which had turned dark again, and added, his voice hushed: "Old Black is the only one who's ever seen it. That's all I have to say on the subject. Enough."

A clap of thunder exploded above them, and the rain came down even harder than before.

"See what I mean!" the old man said. He slowly stood up, his joints creaking.

Liang felt fear as he watched that old face twist into a hard grimace. The eyes were red, the lips blue, the teeth yellow. It was the face of a monster in the flashes of lightning.

"This is it, this is it," the old man murmured, turning to the two apprentices. "Let's take the pots out! It's going to collapse!" He buckled his belt and started for the door.

"No, Master Liu, no! It's too dangerous," one of the young men shouted after him. He and the other apprentice were rooted to the spot.

The old man turned and glared at them until they grudgingly rolled up their sleeves. Then he turned back to the door and took a step.

"No, Grandfather!" Tian shouted, throwing himself at the old man's feet and clinging to one leg. "No! Please don't go out!"

An enormous bolt of lightning dropped from the sky like a ball and rolled across the ground with a deafening roar, trailing fire. The windowpane shattered.

"We must save the kiln," Grandfather Liu said slowly. "It's our life. We have to save it or die with it."

He patted Tian's head, then pushed him away, picked up a big empty sack, and dashed outside. There was another flash of lightning, another clap of thunder, the loudest yet.

The kiln collapsed in a violent crash.

Liang woke up early. Wang had gone out to get breakfast, and Ling was sleeping soundly beside him. He saw by the clock that it was after seven. He wanted to get up, but he was paralyzed by an immense laziness. Then he remembered that he could stay in bed today: school was closed because the children from other villages could not get through the flood.

He lay with his eyes open and tried to remember all the things he had been thinking about before he fell asleep the night before. Grandfather Liu was dead, crushed three days ago under the kiln. Liang shuddered as he recalled the dead man's mangled face, and his own terror and grief. He did not remember coming home. Now his brain seemed frozen in apathy and his limbs were stiff and restless. He fidgeted under the blanket, moving his neck, his fingers, his toes.

His mother came in and put the food on the table.

"Are you awake, Liang?"

"Yes, Mama."

He heard a snap in his body as he sat up. So he lay down again. "Mama," he asked, "is a person taller lying down than standing up?"

"Stupid question," Wang said.

"I think he is," said Liang. "I mean, when you lie down, your joints loosen up, and the bones come apart. Just a little, of course. But they're not jammed together the way they are when you're standing up."

Wang laughed. "So, you feel tall?"

"I do. I've grown in the last three days."

"Well, get up now and eat your breakfast."

Liang dressed and sat on the edge of the bed to feel for his shoes. He heard a voice outside.

"Liang! Are you home?"

It was Tian.

"Yes. Come in."

Tian was an amazing sight. He had a big piece of white cloth wrapped around his head, and his sleeves and shoes had pieces of white cloth on them too.

"You're in mourning for your grandfather?" Wang asked.

"Yes. The burial's today. My father asked me to tell you, Liang; he wants you to come. Grandfather liked you, and he would want you to be there."

"Of course I'll come." Liang wolfed down his breakfast, suddenly feeling important.

"When is it?"

"Now. You'll have to hurry if you want to see him one more time. They're about to close the coffin."

"Oh! I'm ready."

He was about to leave when Wang called to him: "Wait a minute." She took a two-yuan bill out of her pocket and gave it to Liang. "When you go to a funeral, you have to bring a present," she said. "Take this for Grandfather Liu."

Liang put the money in his pocket and ran out with Tian.

They heard wails coming from the Liu house when they were still far off. Reaching the mouth of the alley, they saw four men carrying the body—it was on a stretcher and covered by a big black cloth—toward the street, where a wooden coffin waited. The mourners, dressed in white, followed, now silent.

Tian ran to his father and whispered something to him. Liu turned, saw Liang, then approached an old man and said a few words to him.

The old man looked up. "Wait, Liu," he called out. "Li Liang would like to see Grandfather Liu once more."

The crowd stopped. People turned to look at Liang, and the members of the family, all in white, knelt and moaned loudly.

Liang stood, not sure what to do. The old man came up to him and solemnly asked, "You wish to see him?"

Liang was unable to speak. He nodded.

"I'll give you a mourning cap."

The old man took a piece of white cloth from a bag and wrapped it evenly around Liang's head. An old woman pinned pieces of the same white cloth to his sleeves and around his shoes.

"Go ahead!" the old man said. "Put him down, lift the sheet," he told the pallbearers.

There was a swell of sobbing as the stretcher was set down and the black sheet lifted. The crowd parted for Liang, and everyone waited for him to pay his last respects to the deceased.

Liang was sorry he had asked to see the body. He felt the crowd's eyes on him. He had in fact already seen Grandfather Liu after his death: a mass of blood and torn flesh pulled from the rubble. The nose and mouth had been unrecognizable, and two horrifying mud-filled holes were all that remained of the eyes.

The weeping urged Liang on. He walked hesitantly to the stretcher, and a man lifted the cloth as Liang leaned over. To his surprise, Grandfather Liu's face was not the horror he remembered. The eyes, nose, and mouth were all in place. The dead man looked pale, but serene.

Grandfather Liu seemed to be looking back at him, seemed to be saying, "We must save the kiln."

Liang remembered that they had spoken of the Wen Meng. Had the old man known the monster that made such strange sounds? Had Liang caused the old man's death by saying its name during the storm? Was there some connection between that mysterious noise, the storm, and death? Liang saw no expression of reproach or complaint on the corpse's face, only peace, reminding him of what Grandfather had been when alive: generous to everyone, hard-working, a great teller of tales.

Liang would never hear that wonderful storyteller again. Grandfather's voice had been hoarse, nasal, and he would cough up sticky balls of spit from the back of his throat as he talked, but his stories could make you laugh and cry.

"It's time now."

The man who had uncovered Grandfather's face covered it again. The family's weeping subsided, the bearers lifted the stretcher, and the crowd resumed its slow, silent march to the coffin. Liang walked beside Tian. As he held his friend by the arm, he felt a blood bond forming between them, between him and all the Lius. Grandfather Liu's death was part of it: one drop in an immense family stream.

When they reached the coffin, the crowd stopped again. The family members stood in a close circle around it, friends and acquaintances slightly farther away. An old neighbor, the woman who had consoled Tian's sister Ying on the eve of her wedding, was the first to approach. She placed a gold-embroidered cloth inside and several yuan. As she did so, she chanted:

> *Poor friend, you who all your life were poor,*
> *Take this money with you to your new home. . . .*

When the embroidered cloth was properly spread out, the men lay the body in the coffin. The old aunt put several five-fen coins in the dead man's mouth and slipped two black sticks into his hands. She sang:

> *With these coins, tip the guards of hell,*
> *With these sticks, keep off the dogs that block your path.*
> *Good luck! Good luck, my brother!*

She moved off in tears. Grandmother Liu, the only member of the family not wearing mourning clothes, was the next to approach. She examined everything meticulously, her eyes filled with tears. The body was covered with a silver cloth. When the men placed the cover on the coffin, the old woman began to weep:

> *My dear, I cannot believe*
> *That here we must say farewell.*

The man handed Liu a hammer. As the deceased's eldest son, he had to put the first nail in the coffin. Tian's father, ordinarily so strong and brave, seemed barely able to lift his arm, much less drive in the nail. Grandmother Liu began to weep.

> *Fifty-five years ago, I was a girl in yellow.*
> *You took me from my mother's home.*
> *It was here you first took me by the hand.*
> *You led me across mighty rivers, yet now*
> *In this little stream your vessel sinks.*

After striking a few blows, Liu handed the hammer to Tian, who started on the second nail. "Rest in peace, Grandfather, rest in peace," he murmured, just as his father had.

Unable to finish, he dissolved in tears and dropped the hammer.

The crowd burst into tears as well. The wailing of the women, the moaning of the men, and the blows of the hammer as the pallbearers nailed the coffin lid filled the street, echoed to the sky.

When the coffin was sealed, a despairing Grandmother Liu left for home alone. She was not allowed to attend her husband's burial.

At that moment a tall boy arrived, went to the man who seemed to be directing things, and said, "Uncle Old Black says the funeral may begin."

"Then let it begin!" the man declared.

The Liu family lined up on either side of the coffin, men on the left, women on the right. They all knelt and touched their heads to the ground. The villagers began to come, divided according to sex, to offer their condolences. Weeping loudly, they stated their relationship to the deceased. It was their last opportunity to communicate with him.

"We thank you on the family's behalf," the leader exclaimed as each group finished paying its respects, and the members of the Liu family bowed three times to the visitors.

Then it was the turn of relatives from other villages to present their gifts. Those who lived closest brought food for an eight-course meal; those more distant brought white sheets inscribed with the words *Eternal Soul* or *Happiness As High As the Sky*. For two or three yuan, they bought pieces of white cloth for mourning armbands, then took their places behind the family.

Liu, now the family elder, approached the coffin to address his father publicly for the last time. Unable to speak, he knelt, slapped his hands on the ground, and wept, a heart-rending sound.

Then it was his wife's turn. She, too, knelt beside the coffin:

> *O great heaven! I became your child.*
> *It was you who taught me to be a woman,*
> *And now you abandon me.*

She touched her head to the ground and tore her hair in despair. The women wept with her.

Tian's cousins, male and female, whom Liang had met at the wedding, also wept as they filed past the coffin. But Tian's tears were the saddest of all. His skinny body, huddled in the middle of the street, his childish voice, hoarse from all the crying, his weakness and loneliness, all seemed to bring memories of the times the old man had led his grandson by the hand through the streets, in the fields, or around his potter's kiln.

"To mourn the dead is to mourn oneself." Liang had heard that saying often enough, but had never understood it. Now, as he watched this throng of mourners give voice to their grief, he felt as though he were watching a play. The actors struck the ground, tore their hair, and cried out, as if deliberately clinging to the pain caused by Grandfather Liu's death, as if somehow it stood for the pain of life itself. Liang thought that deep within each peasant lay a hidden well of tears, which gushed to the surface for this ceremony.

The weeping went on all morning. When the sun hung high overhead and the meal was finished, the procession set off for the cemetery. Whelk players led the march, blowing into their ancient instruments, whose melancholy sound seemed to mimic voices both dead and living, seemed to call up all the sorrows of man and nature and the poor yellow earth.

Next came the children, with many-colored paper cut-outs representing legendary heroes. The children waved them while firecrackers exploded all around.

Liu, a paper veil draped over his shoulders, walked behind the cart while his wife, seated in the cart behind the coffin, tossed coin-shaped pieces of paper to ward off hatred and misfortune.

The convoy, in an immense whirlwind of yellow dust, in a river of shrieks and tears, in bursts of color and deafening explosions from the fireworks, made its way from this world to the one beyond, to the world of the dead, the place called Yin. The encounter of the mourners with the beings of the world of Yin would be celebrated like the meeting of two armies, each striving to display its power and its will.

The cemetery lay east of the village, in an isolated spot under a twisted tree. The graves were visible from far off, lined up proudly. They were arranged like a family tree: the oldest ancestor, greatest and most venerable, commanded from the top; his increasingly numerous descendants stood below him like soldiers awaiting orders.

The procession arrived and the pallbearers lowered the coffin into the hole; the leader issued instructions, his eyes fixed southward, into the distance, as though seeking the gateway to the beyond.

Liu dropped in the first handful of earth. Then everyone else made his contribution for Grandfather's new home. Afterward, the women ran back to the village—ran, since tradition held that the first to return would have a son to replace the man the family had lost.

Liang stood beside Tian during the burial, wept and dropped earth on the coffin like a member of the family. He felt very close to Grandfather, who in death seemed more present than ever.

The sun sank slowly, the crowd of mourners dispersed through the fields, and the graves resumed their silence as the dead welcomed their new neighbor.

Liang turned and cast a last glance at the fresh grave. "Good-bye, Grandfather Liu," he said.

十九

All the work was worth it.

Summer passed, with its drought and floods. But thanks to the leadership of the Party Commune Committee, the Xin Zhuang district brought in an exceptional harvest that autumn. With their granaries full and their courtyards rich with hay, the peasants had nothing but praise for the Party.

There had been a lot to the old saying "If Xin Zhuang has a good harvest, even a dog can marry a beautiful woman." Now, the villagers built new houses, planned marriages for their children, and began to dream of the birth of new heirs. In the midst of this prosperity, the district was dazzled by one event in particular: the arrival of electricity.

Liang and Tian were a little sad when they heard the news.

"Too bad we weren't the first to produce it," said Liang, taking his friend by the arm as they walked to the commune threshing floor. That was where the first electric light was to be demonstrated.

A shadow passed across Tian's face. But he said confidently, "Don't worry. We can be first with something else."

"Like what?"

"An opera box."

"A what?"

"A box that can talk and sing," Tian said, his eyes shining. "I read about it in a book."

"It's called radio," Liang explained.

They began to map out magnificent projects again, and were still deep in conversation when they arrived at the threshing floor, where a large crowd had already gathered amid the sorghum stalks. A tall young man with a serious air was surrounded by peasants, some seated, some standing. He had a lot of equipment with him and was preparing the installation.

"Stand back," he said, waving irritably at people who got too close to him. "This can kill you."

The offended villagers took a few steps back and sat down near the piles of stalks.

"Will that thing really light up, with just those iron wires and no oil?" asked a little old man with a dirty beard. His cheeks caved in as he sucked heavily on his pipe.

"Strange," said the young man sitting next to him, stroking his hairless chin with a knowing air. "At first I thought the iron wires were hollow, so oil could flow through and light the lamp. But I checked, and they aren't."

"It will be a good joke if it doesn't work," said the old man. He shook his head with a mischievous look and stroked his beard with the clay stem of his pipe.

Liang was laughing inside. He waited impatiently for the triumph of science, anxious to see how these villagers would react to the impossible.

"I told you to keep away from it," the electrician yelled at a boy. "Especially the wire. It can kill."

The boy moved into the crowd, muttering, "He's so conceited. Three months' training in town and he thinks he's a wizard."

"Oh, stop," one of his friends said. "There's nothing you can do about it. He who enters the temple becomes a monk. You and I will never set foot in the temple, because work in the fields is all we're good for. You were born under an unlucky star, that's all."

"He acts like it'll work," someone else said. "But it just isn't possible."

The electrician finished installing his equipment and asked a boy to go to the neighboring village and tell them to turn the current on. The boy set off at a run, and everyone waited.

The wait seemed interminable. The sun had set long ago, night had fallen, and still the bulb was dark.

The crowd became restless.

"I think I'll go home," said the little old man with the dirty beard. "I don't want to waste my evening on this foolishness. I could have stayed home and made jasmine tea, and now I'd be sitting on my nice warm bed, legs crossed, smoking my Shandong tobacco."

He took the pipe out of his mouth, tapped it against the sole of his shoe, spat on the sparks that fell, and straightened as if to rise. But instead he only shifted on his rump, refilled his pipe, and lit it. "I should go home," he muttered.

The young man beside him fidgeted too, changing his position in the sorghum straw. "As the old proverb says," he commented, rubbing his chin again, 'No hair on the chin, sand in the works.' I bet he brought the wrong wire."

Liang felt a burning sensation, as if it was his fault the bulb had not gone on. He slapped his thigh, thinking: Come on, electricity. Please light the bulb. Show them what science is. Please!

"What's the matter?" Tian asked him.

"Nothing. And what's the matter with you? Your hand's shaking."

"It is not," said Tian in a choked voice.

But Liang saw tears in his friend's eyes.

Just when everyone was about to lose hope, the bulb burst into dazzling light. Liang could have sworn it gave a little jump first. Most of the villagers gasped and threw up their hands, as if to repel an attack.

"Oh!"

Then everyone rushed up to the bulb, squinting at it and blinking.

"It's blinding!" said the old man, peering through his fingers.

"I'm not going to give up my oil lamp for that thing," said the young man. "It'll ruin my wife's eyes."

Liang and Tian were ecstatic. They joined the crowd, which now was circling the bulb in a joyous uproar.

Suddenly Tian grabbed Liang's arm and pointed at an insect on the ground. "See that?" he said.

"Yes. What about it?"

"It's very good to eat."

"What? That black grasshopper?"

"Yes. One day, my grandfather caught three of them, and my grandmother fried them. They were delicious."

"Look, another one!" Liang cried, pointing. "And another one!"

"Look up!"

A swarm of insects fluttered in the light above the crowd, spinning in luminous circles. They flew around the bulb and dive-bombed the villagers, who, not understanding the reason for the attack, thought some practical joker was throwing the insects. They grabbed the living bullets and hurled them back. A battle began.

"Let's catch some," Tian said. Hurriedly he took off his pants and tied the legs together, making a sack with two long pockets. He ran around the room gathering grasshoppers. Liang joined in.

As the young peasants battled, for the game had begun to degenerate into fistfights, the two boys filled their sack with the curious delicacies. Tian, his bottom bare, the sack on his shoulder, and with Liang guarding him, started home. They made up a mocking song as they walked:

> *Whether you believe or don't, it doesn't matter!*
> *The doors of science are open now.*
> *We'll plow without oxen, light lamps without oil.*
> *While you fight, we're going to have a treat.*

At the house, Tian's grandmother helped them remove the shells of the black grasshoppers and wash the insects in salt water to clean out their insides. Then she put them on to fry, but the boys insisted on tasting them before the cooking was done.

Liang sat on the floor of the Liu family's living room, his legs folded under him. He ate noisily, smiling at his friend.

Tian wanted more entertainment. "Grandmother," he asked with his mouth full, "why don't you tell us a story?"

"Yes. That's a good idea!" Liang put in.

Grandmother Liu had become milder, more talkative since her husband's death. She was only too happy to carry out the boys' request. Her toothless mouth chomped as she began her story in a monotone, her voice far away.

"It was long, long ago, back in the days when contests were held to see who would become a mandarin or a prime minister. In autumn, after the harvest, all the scholars of the country, rich and poor, from the cities and from the villages, would travel to the capital to compete.

"One day, two young men met on the road from the west. One was dressed in silk and wore shoes of leather. He had a rosy complexion, and his eyes were bright. He rode on a grand horse. The other, his body covered with rags, was pale and thin. He was barefoot, and his back was bent. Despite the difference between them, they became friends. Equally knowledgeable and intelligent, they talked first about history. One would ask difficult questions; the other would answer with confidence. From history they went to literature. One would speak on a difficult theme; the other would improvise a clever poem. Finally they had exhausted every topic. But their journey was far from over, and they liked each other so well that it would have been a shame not to continue their conversation.

" 'Well,' the rich man began, 'what do you think of life?'

" 'Life in what sense?'

" 'Our life. How we should live. Whether we should be good or evil.'

" 'An interesting question!' the poor man said. 'All the books we read tell us that we should lead a good life, that we should have a good heart, do good deeds. And yet . . .'

"Until then, his friend had listened with approval. But now he frowned and asked: 'What do you mean, *and yet*?'

" 'And yet,' the man on foot continued, casting a sly glance at his friend, 'although it is an easy thing to say and to ask of others, when it comes to applying it in practice, it's not so simple.'

" 'Why is that?' asked the man on horseback.

" 'I don't know, but it is so. Sometimes I wonder if the books are right.'

" 'What you say is very serious,' the rich man replied, shocked. 'How can you question books, which we must always respect, in all circumstances?'

"But the poor man seemed determined to argue with his friend. 'Yes,' he said, 'it is a very serious thing to say. But history shows, and it is just as true today, that those who try to be good come to wretched ends, whereas those who act wickedly are crowned with success.'

" 'And what do you conclude from this?' asked the horseman in a threatening voice, prepared to defend the sacred idea of Confucius at any cost.

" 'I must conclude,' said the poor man, 'that in this life it is better to be wicked than to be good.'

" 'Now you go too far,' the furious horseman said, and a great debate began. Each gave examples from history, used all his erudition, but he could not convince the other.

"Just then they noticed an old man tilling the field not far from the road.

" 'Let's let him decide,' said the rich man. 'If he agrees with you, I will give you my horse and fine clothes; if he agrees with me, however, I will ask nothing of you.'

"They approached the old man, greeted him politely, and asked their question.

"The old man listened carefully and thought for a long time, as though consulting the Great Lord of Heaven. 'Since my earliest youth,' he replied, 'I was told that we must be good, and that is how I lived my life. But now that I am old and near death, I believe it is better to be wicked.'

"The rich man kept his word, giving his horse and fine clothes to his friend. But still he was not satisfied. This time he wagered his money, and the two put the same question to a man coming toward them pushing a wheelbarrow.

"Alas, the poor man won again. He took his friend's money.

" 'Let us wager one last time,' the loser said, seeing a child of twelve by the road. 'If the child is against me, I will be convinced.'

" 'You have nothing left to wager,' said the winner, now dressed in silk and seated on the grand horse.

"The loser thought for a moment. 'If you win again,' he said, 'I will let you put out my eyes.'

"So they asked the child the question. The child replied instantly, 'It is better to be wicked.'

"The winner then dismounted, took a knife, and put out his friend's eyes."

Liang and Tian were astounded by the story and anxious to hear what happened next. But just at that moment, Liu walked in. When he saw how tired his mother looked, he scolded the boys.

"Let Grandmother get some rest now," he said.

The boys, dejected, had no choice.

"I'll tell you the end some other time," said Grandmother.

PART TWO

"Revolution . . ."

"Cultural Revolution . . ."

"Great Cultural Revolution . . ."

The sun hung high in a clear sky, but it moved laboriously. It cast as much light as it did in summer, but its touch on the land below was remote and indifferent, its sparkle too pure, almost icy.

"Let us raise high the proud red flag of Mao Zedong Thought and carry the Great Proletarian Cultural Revolution through to the end. . . ."

The north wind tore wildly through the village, leaping from alley to alley. Like a fury with a thousand invisible arms, it lashed the leafless trees, which fought back with their fragile dry branches, until they snapped with shrill, painful cries. It was a hopeless battle.

The cold seemed to seep from the blue sky, from the howling wind, from the nooks and crannies of the low houses, from cracks in the earth. Sometimes it took a twisted path, throwing up whirlwinds, and it missed no opportunity to slip under collars, and up sleeves of padded jackets, and to attack ankles with its sharp tongue.

When the sky was clear, it was even colder.

"We are now engaged in a struggle to the death for our revolutionary cause. We cannot afford the slightest faintness of heart, the slightest weakness. . . ."

"A revolution is not a dinner party, or

writing an essay, or painting a picture, or doing embroidery. . . . A revolution is an insurrection, an act of violence, by which one class overthrows another. . . ."

Loudspeakers recently installed in all villages blared spirited messages through the chill and the sun's dazzling light. The north wind carried the words far and wide.

Liang, charmed by the revolutionary voice, did not think about the cold. He was walking slowly, his back bowed like a little old man's, each hand buried in the opposite sleeve. In his thick, baggy cotton pants, he looked like a clown in a traditional comic opera. All I need is a little patch of white on the tip of my nose and some black shadow on my eyelids, he thought. His cotton-stuffed clogs slapped loudly on the frozen ground.

He liked listening to the loudspeaker. It was a mark of progress, an achievement of the Revolution. One night, not long after electricity came, when he was still marveling at how the village looked all lit up, he had found his father at home but in the middle of a meeting with the Committee.

"The next step will be to install electric pumps for the wells," his father was saying, swallowing with a noticeable movement of his Adam's apple, which betrayed uneasiness.

"Yes," Song replied, "and we could also set up those big electric trumpets—in the highest places, so the sound will carry."

"They're called loudspeakers," Zhao Jialu said, laughing.

"I know," Song murmured, embarrassed. "That's what I meant. Loudspeakers. With them, we can drown out all other sounds and that way reach into the hearts of our villagers more directly. We can transmit Party directives to them immediately and with great force."

And that was the origin of the thundering voices that had dominated the district ever since.

"Our great leader Chairman Mao teaches us that though the laws of Marxism number in the thousands, they can be summed up in a single law. To rebel is justified. . . ."

So spoke Liang's cousin, Brother Number Two, imitating the loudspeaker but with a funny Peking accent.

I wonder if he knows what Marxism is, or what "rebel" means, Liang thought.

It was only that morning that he had met Brother Number Two, a son of his uncle on his father's side. Liang's mother had waked him up early. "Liang, hurry up," she had said. "Brother Number Two has come for you."

When Liang opened his eyes, he saw a tall boy with broad shoulders and sunburned face, maybe seventeen, groping for words.

"Your aunt sent me to get you," he finally said in a husky voice.

During supper one evening, Liang's father had talked about the spring holiday in his native village, about the old customs and practices. Liang, fascinated, had expressed a desire to spend his spring holiday in that village, with his uncles, cousins, the whole Li family.

"I'll see what I can do," his father had said.

Now his cousin had really come for him. Liang leaped out of bed, threw on his clothes, and shared his breakfast with his cousin. Grabbing the sack his mother had got ready for him, he left immediately, forgetting to say good-bye to Wang and Ling. He didn't give a thought to Tian, either, which he would regret later, though not with any great remorse.

The strong wind made the boys stumble and bump into

each other. They smiled. His cousin had dark eyes, eyebrows shaped like willow leaves, and big yellow teeth. Liang felt like putting his arms around this tall boy. They had the same grandfather, so they were linked by a firm, invisible bond.

"Brother Number Two," Liang murmured in a timid voice.

"Yes?"

Liang blushed, not sure exactly how to phrase his question. "How many days is it to the spring holiday?"

Brother Number Two thought for a moment, then answered in the tone of a wise old man: "Let's see. Today's Cold Eight, the holiday of the twelfth month of the lunar calendar, when we celebrate the departure of the Lord of the Hearth and his wife to heaven. That means it's seven days to the spring holiday."

"The Lord of the Hearth and his wife fly to heaven?"

"Yes. All year long they watch what we do in the house, they keep track of the bad things and the good things. Then they fly away to report to the Great Lord of Heaven."

"And then what?" Liang asked, eager to know more.

"Then, if the family has done too many bad things during the year, heaven punishes them."

"How can heaven punish them?" Liang asked, looking up at the constantly changing sky, the pale white faces of the clouds rushing by.

"With storms, for one thing. I'll give you an example. Three years ago, a boy raped his grandmother in a village near ours. The next day, a bolt of lightning came out of a perfectly clear sky and cut him in two. And it was winter, when there aren't any storms."

"Really?" an astonished Liang asked. He was silent for

a while. "And how do you send the Lord of the Hearth and his wife up to heaven?"

"With fire, of course," his cousin answered, growing impatient with Liang's ignorance. "We burn them."

We burn them. . . .

Fire burned in the Li family's hearth. They were all present in the icy night, kneeling before dancing flames that quickly swallowed the dried straw collected for this sacred moment.

In his peasant fingers—thick, coarse, and dirty—Uncle Li, the patriarch, held two painted figures of poor-quality paper, their colors faded by the hundreds of days they had spent hanging by the hearth in dust, smoke, and spiderwebs. The Lord of the Hearth and his wife were dressed in red. The Lord, who had a black beard, long and thin, was smiling sweetly, almost meekly. His wife had bright red lips and a tender look.

In the deep silence of that solemn moment, Uncle Li took a piece of candy shaped like a small melon and placed it in the Lord's mouth. Then he put the figure into the flames, singing:

> *May your mercy, your kindness, be boundless!*
> *Eat this sweet cake, and may your mouth be sweet*
> *When you speak of us in heaven.*

The family members, still kneeling, touched their foreheads to the ground. Liang did not know how to kneel properly, so he watched, fascinated, yet skeptical.

The fire's many tongues licked at the Lord of the Hearth, then suddenly devoured him in a single gulp. The figure turned black, spitting a strange blue flame. The candy was gone.

Liang's aunt picked up the figure of the Lord's wife, traditionally called Grandmother of the Hearth. She placed several pieces of candy in the figure's mouth, then put it in the flames, her hands shaking. She sang too:

> *Grandmother of the Hearth,*
> *Who observes our acts through the year*
> *With a keen and kindly eye,*
> *In them you will find only goodness.*
> *Today we hail your departure,*
> *But will see you again when the new year comes.*
> *Tell the Great Lord of Heaven the truth,*
> *Grant our children good companions,*
> *Give us the rich harvest we so desire. . . .*

She has a lot more to say, Liang thought. He looked at his aunt, a small woman with a wrinkled face and gray hair, and noticed her kind eyes, which were now filled with tears.

When the Lord of the Hearth and his wife had flown off on their journey, the members of the family rose. Everyone was now entitled to a piece of candy: a precious moment that came but once a year.

Like all his cousins, Liang got a piece of candy. He put it in his mouth and stood riveted, staring at the fire that had consumed the figures. Their silhouettes were becoming twisted, fragile. The heavy paper—the bodies of the Lord and his wife—changed color: from red to yellow, then to blazing white, then red again, then yellow and black, and finally the dull white of death and nothingness. The Lord and his wife both vanished in smoke that rose from under the bed of hard-packed earth, the warm earth on which the whole family gathered to sleep each night. The smoke passed through a long narrow black pipe into the pure cold air of the night.

The Lord and his wife, arm in arm, soared to the heavenly palace, their mouths full of sugar, hers more than his. They began their report to the Great Lord of Heaven: "The Li, Yang, and Liu families have been good and honest. Others, however, have acted selfishly and wickedly."

The Great Lord of Heaven listened with his eyes closed, his toothless jaws working steadily. With an indifferent air, he calculated the rewards he would bestow upon the good and the punishment he would inflict upon the wicked.

Liang wondered, with sudden anxiety, what would happen to him, to his father, his mother, his little sister? How would they be judged, they who had no lords in their hearth, who didn't even have a hearth, and therefore no celestial messenger to speak on their behalf? Would the Great Lord number them among the good or among the wicked? Would he grant them his protection? Maybe the Great Lord doesn't even know we exist, Liang thought. How sad it would be, to be cut off from this world like that, to live without roots, to be like a brook without a source, like leaves torn from a blackened branch and scattered by the wind!

Liang felt very lonely. He looked with pleading eyes at the dying embers, wishing he could rescue some tiny fragment of the Lord of the Hearth. He wanted to explain who he was, to tell him about his family, about the Communist Party and the wells his father had ordered dug, the good harvest they had had, the coming of electricity, the Cultural Revolution, and the people's happiness. And about his own ambition to become a hero, to follow the difficult yet glorious path his father and grandfather had blazed for him.

二十一

A week later came the spring holiday.

The day before was the most hectic day of the whole year. The village was in turmoil; people were milling grain, making omelettes, killing pigs and chickens, cooking meat, and baking bread. The streets were filled with shouts, smells, and smoke. The excitement was punctuated by fireworks set off by children proudly displaying their new clothes.

"Liang," said Uncle Li, "I want you to go with Brother Number Two and buy some red paper. Then you both can write little signs for us to hang around the house."

Liang, dazzled by all the animation, was delighted to be of use in the holiday preparations.

"We should also buy a portrait of Chairman Mao," commented Brother Number One. He was the secretary of the local Party cell.

"And some Lords of the Hearth too," added Aunt Li.

Uncle Li hesitated. "How much is all that going to cost?" he asked, wallet in hand.

"At least thirty fen," said Brother Number Two.

"Out of the question," his father exclaimed. "I spent twenty fen for the Lord's departure to heaven, and I have only fifty fen left."

"I have twenty fen!" Liang cried, reaching into his pocket for the money Wang had given him.

"Oh, that's wonderful!" They were overjoyed.

Liang handed the money to his cousin, who took a ten-fen bill from his father.

In the street they ran into a neighbor, known as Uncle Hammer. He was carrying a package under his arm.

"The shop's still open, isn't it, Uncle Hammer?" Liang's cousin asked the old man.

"It is. Look," he said, showing the boys his red paper.

"Did you buy some Lords of the Hearth too?" Liang asked, proud that he now knew all about this custom.

Old Uncle Hammer did not answer immediately. He looked solemn. "It's a great sin to talk that way, little boy," he said. "How can you use the word 'buy' to refer to such a holy act?"

"You're supposed to say 'invite,' " Brother Number Two whispered.

Liang blushed. "Well," he said, trying to save face, "how much did it cost you to invite these lords?"

"These lords?" The old man held his package out abruptly, as though he meant to give it to Liang. He looked at the boys through dark, lifeless eyes. "I paid more than twenty fen for all this shit," he suddenly said.

Then he spun around and walked off, heading for home, the roll of paper sticking out like a tail growing from his armpit. He hopped a little.

The cousins, stunned, watched him for a moment, then burst out laughing.

At the small village shop they bought red paper, a portrait of Chairman Mao, and two figures for the hearth.

When they got home, Liang's aunt took the Lord and his wife and hung them respectfully and carefully on the fireplace. Liang and Brother Number Two cut the red paper into squares and long rectangles.

"What should I write, Uncle?" Liang asked when they were ready.

"The usual."

"What's the usual?"

"What's the matter with you? What do they teach you in school?" his aunt chided jokingly. "Just look at the boy: he seems intelligent enough, but in fact he's getting stupider and stupider from all that reading."

The whole family laughed, including Liang.

"Look at what we wrote last year," his uncle said, pointing to the wall above the big bed and to the doors.

That was when Liang first noticed the faded, dusty signs, difficult to make out against the earth wall. He was able to decipher, "May this home be filled with sons!"

There were two signs on the bedroom door. On the right: "A dry log, fine rice, and a tight roof."

On the left: "Good health, strength, and great joy."

Above the bedroom door: "Great peace."

There were three on the front door. To the right: "Neither theft nor violence; an honest family." To the left: "Neither lend nor borrow; rely on your own strength." And between, higher: "Wisdom protects us."

"Do I have to write all that?" Liang asked.

"Yes," Uncle Li answered. "Those are the family mottoes."

Liang copied them, faithfully imitating the characters, even though he did not understand the meaning of all the phrases.

"Where am I supposed to put the portrait of Chairman Mao?" Liang's aunt suddenly asked. "Next to the Lord of the Hearth?"

"Yes, I guess so," muttered Uncle Li, embarrassed.

"But then there'll be two men and only one woman," Aunt Li protested. "That's not fair."

"You're right," Uncle Li admitted. "They don't sell Mao's wife, do they?" he asked his son.

"No. And even if they did, we don't have enough money."

"What do I do?" Aunt Li shrugged her shoulders.

"We'd better ask our older boy. He's the one who got us into this complicated business."

Moments later Brother Number One came home. Everyone recognized his footsteps by the sound of his Japanese shoes. "What's the matter?" he asked as he came in.

"We don't know where to put this portrait of Mao."

"Right there in front of you, on the north wall," Brother Number One said with the knowing look of a Party cell secretary.

His mother hung the portrait.

"What are you writing, Liang?"

"Holiday signs," Uncle Li answered for Liang.

"What, those ancient sayings?" asked Brother Number One.

"Yes. They're the family mottoes."

Liang stopped writing.

"No. Out of the question. Impossible," exclaimed Brother Number One. "Times have changed. We can't put such stuff up anymore. I'm a Party cadre in this village, and my uncle's a prefect. Only revolutionary slogans go up. In the past few days the radio's been talking about nothing but the Great Cultural Revolution. Something's going on at the top."

Uncle Li's face changed completely. Looking scared, he waved his hand.

"Whatever you say," he said. "We'll write whatever you want."

Liang looked admiringly at Brother Number One, who scratched his head before he began to dictate.

"Above the bed: 'Revolutionary household.'"

"On the bedroom door: 'Study hard! Never forget the Party! If we have happiness, it is thanks to Chairman Mao!'"

"To the right of the front door: 'Renounce life and scorn death! Make the Revolution!'"

"To the left: 'Follow the path of Chairman Mao, climbing the mountain of knives, crossing the sea of fire!'"

"And above the door: 'To rebel is justified.'"

Liang listened, rapt, as Brother Number One spoke. Groping for the right characters, he wrote in his child's hand, with all the enthusiastic strength his ten years could muster. He did not understand all of it, but he knew that what he was writing was wonderful and that it expressed the ideal to which his father was devoted day and night, the ideal for which his grandfather had died a hero. And Liang would do the same, would devote his entire life to it.

The first pieces of bread stuffed with meat were ready around noon. When Liang's aunt took the cover off the pot, a cloud of steam rose up and a tantalizing smell filled the house. The bread, dazzling white and flower-shaped, made Liang hungry. All the writing had given him an appetite. Not waiting for the bread to cool off, he grabbed a piece and was about to pop it into his mouth when his aunt stopped him.

"No," she said. "We can't eat New Year's bread until the lords and our ancestors have eaten."

She took a place, put several steaming pieces of bread on it, and set it in front of the new Lord of the Hearth and his wife. Casting a furtive glance at Chairman Mao, she picked out four more pieces, wrapped them in cloth, and said to Liang in a confidential tone, "Please go with Brother Number Two and give these to your grandparents."

"My grandparents?" Liang blurted out. "But they're dead!"

"That's right, you have to take these to their graves. I know you town people don't like this kind of thing, but it's only right for you to perform this task. When your grandparents were alive, you and your father were their favorites. Then your father went off to make the Revolution and was never able to spend the New Year with the family. And he has never visited their graves. Well, he can be forgiven for that, because he's a prefect. But this is the first time you've spent the holiday with us, and it would be a great pleasure for your grandparents if you brought them this food. You represent your father here."

Liang swelled with pride at the idea of representing his father. He took the package of stuffed bread. Just before he and his cousin set out for the cemetery, Aunt Li handed them a wad of bills from "the bank of the beyond" and whispered to Liang's cousin, "Don't show these to your older brother, or he'll scold me."

On their way the boys met many peasants who had just performed the same rite. Backs bowed in the cold, they seemed very serious, as though they had just spoken to their deceased relatives.

At the cemetery, Liang's cousin looked around for a while before he spotted their grandparents' graves. "There," he said.

He knelt, placed the bread on the graves, and set fire to the fake money, muttering words Liang could not make out.

Liang, thinking that this was silly, was not sure what to do.

"Aren't you going to greet our grandparents?" his cousin asked, surprised.

"Yes," Liang answered, crouching down beside him. He took a stick and began to stir the fire. He found that fun.

"You're not crying?" he asked, remembering the burial of Grandfather Liu.

"No," his cousin replied. "That's for women."

The paper money burned quickly. Liang watched as the bills became ash and were carried away by the wind, swirling higher and higher in the sky above them. He thought maybe his grandparents, whom he had never seen, were hidden somewhere in the air and were delighted to receive this money and a visit from their favorite grandson.

When the flames had died, Brother Number Two, still kneeling, took a piece of bread. "Eat while it's still hot," he said to Liang with his mouth full.

"Isn't that a lack of respect for our grandparents?" Liang asked, taking a piece of bread anyway. He was very hungry.

"No, not at all," said his cousin. "The dead don't eat. We bring them the first bread of the year as a token of respect. But there's nothing to stop us from eating it afterward. It's really good!"

Brother Number Two swallowed another mouthful. Liang ate too. The meat-stuffed bread was delicious.

The sun set into a bed of rosy clouds. Night fell rapidly, to the joyful shouts of the boys in the village. They were having a fireworks contest, hurling their little explosives as high as possible. The sky blazed with sparks. The girls, not allowed to set off firecrackers, lit colorful Chinese lanterns shaped like roosters, butterflies, frogs. Nearly all the girls wore red. In groups of four or five, they threaded their way through the crowds. When firecrackers went off above their heads, they screamed and ran.

The houses were lit with hundreds of lanterns, newly made or taken out of storage. Families gathered on their wide earth beds and ate dumplings, the traditional meal, symbol of the warmth of coming together.

Shouts, lights, wonderful smells—that was the holiday.

But, above it all, the loudspeakers blared, in this and all the other villages of the district:

"The Cultural Revolution . . ."

First and second Nine,
* don't take out your hands.*
Third and fourth Nine, walk on ice.
Fifth Nine, the rivers thaw, don't thaw.
Sixth Nine, the swallows return,
* don't return.*

The voice, as frail and shrill as a cracked Chinese violin, came from the end of a sloping alley.

Liang went toward the voice and saw a little girl dressed in red. She was rocking a baby in her arms. The nursery rhyme seemed to come from her two ribboned braids, which bounced back and forth like sticks beating an imaginary drum.

Seventh and eighth Nine,
* if we don't work the earth,*
We'll all get mad for nothing
When the ninth Nine comes.

The melody stirred Liang's memory. Grandmother Liu had taught him that old song. It made him feel good to hum it. But suddenly he stopped. Might it not be a crime to sing it now? For some time—ever since his return from that wonderful holiday with his cousins—Liang had had the feeling that things were changing.

The Cultural Revolution: everyone was talking about it, including Liang.

The loudspeaker, first of all. Then the little red holiday signs. And people at meetings. At home, Liang had noticed that the words came often to his father's lips, and that his father was buoyed by them.

"What's the Cultural Revolution?" Liang had asked after telling his parents all about the visit to his uncle's village.

"You'll find out soon," Li had answered in a solemn, guarded voice, as if proud of the maturity shown by his son's question. But Liang had been disappointed by the way his father evaded it.

"The Great Cultural Revolution, the Great . . ."

His little sister, Ling, had repeated the words in her tinkly voice when she played with her doll. She didn't seem much a child anymore. It was as if she had caught up to Liang in the few days she had spent alone with their parents.

Liang had set about getting information, explanations. But he was careful not to let his ignorance be too obvious. He questioned Tian, Liu, his mother, even his sister. He tried to find out something from Grandmother Song. But the answers were always vague, obscure, spoken in a mysterious tone. At last he realized that everybody was almost as ignorant as he was.

But today he had heard the long-awaited explanation, officially. Normal classes at school had been interrupted as they always were when something important was happening, and the principal had addressed all the students:

"We are now in the midst of a red period. Red means revolutionary. As our Great Leader Chairman Mao has said, 'We can attain our ideal of Communism—our sole ideal—only by waging a permanent and unrelenting class struggle to bury capitalism definitively.'

"That is why we must make this Revolution, which will last throughout our socialist epoch.

"This Revolution is called the Great Cultural Revolution. It will be carried out in several stages. The first may be summed up this way:

"We must uproot the Four Olds: old traditions, old customs, old habits, and old ways of thinking.

"In their place we must lay down the Four New Traditions. . . ."

That nursery rhyme is surely one of the old things that must be uprooted, Liang now thought as he watched the little girl in red. He was proud to have understood his error, and to have corrected it so quickly, thereby proving himself worthy of Chairman Mao's precepts, and worthy to be a prefect's son.

Liang took long strides down the narrow alley, his hands in his pockets, his fingers toying with the two bills his mother had just given him.

"Can I take this money, Mama?" he'd said. "I have to go right away, before they're sold out."

"Take it. And hurry!"

His mother had never given him money so easily. But it was natural, because this time he was not going to buy some little thing—candy, fruit, a notebook, a pencil, or a comic book. This time it was a very, very important thing.

Liang left the alley and turned right at the main street, heading straight for the shop. He took the money out of his right pocket and transferred it to his left. He touched it, felt it, caressed those bills that had been so often crumpled, fingered, handled. They had been used to buy vegetables, straw, socks, and countless other commonplace things. Shopkeepers had given them in change a thousand times, they had passed from hand to hand, finally winding up in Wang's purse and then in Liang's pocket, first the right pocket, then the left.

And to think that soon—in just a few minutes—Liang

would exchange this money for something far more precious, something essential, the only possession that was important.

He quickened his step, trying to look like an adult. He saw the shop ahead, its door open like a hungry mouth, its windows closed and shuttered like blind eyes. He remembered all the times he had gone there with a few fen, begged to buy an apple, some jujubes, or a couple of pieces of candy that had to be shared with his sister. But not today.

He crossed the threshold and found himself face to face with the bald shopkeeper, who smiled broadly, flashing his gold teeth. This seemed like an insult; the stupid man must have thought Liang had come in for some silly child's treat, as usual.

And something else bothered Liang. Why was this ordinary shop the place where they sold what he had come to buy, which was such an important, serious, venerable thing? He was offended.

"How are you, Liang?" asked the shopkeeper, rubbing his stubbly chin.

"All right," Liang murmured, a little sullen. "I came to buy . . ."

The shopkeeper's smile faded, and suddenly he looked very serious. He must have seen from Liang's face that this was no common errand.

"That!" Liang concluded, pointing to the very center of a shelf covered with precious red cloth, bright and splendid, a red deeper than blood itself.

"The Little Red Book?" the shopkeeper inquired in a deferential tone.

"*Quotations from Chairman Mao*," Liang said, in the tone his father used whenever the subject came up.

The shopkeeper hurried to the gleaming red cloth and

carefully picked up the volume in the center. With both hands he offered it ceremoniously to Liang.

Liang took it with the greatest care. To his surprise, it weighed much less than he expected.

He hurriedly paid and left the store, grasping the red book tightly in both hands.

"Liang, did you buy *Quotations from Chairman Mao* too?"

He did not have to turn around: he knew that voice, as piercing as clashing cymbals, all too well: Grandmother Song's.

"Yes, Grandmother."

His little sister, dressed in red, stood beside the old woman, eating a pancake.

"We bought the Little Red Book the day before yesterday, when it first went on sale," Grandmother Song bragged. "Why don't you recite a paragraph for your brother," she said to Ling.

Ling reluctantly took the pancake out of her mouth. Hesitating, she looked uneasily at the old woman.

"Go ahead," Grandmother insisted. "Recite the paragraph we just learned by heart from your aunt."

Ling still hesitated, her mouth full of pancake, her eyes squinting in the rays of the setting sun.

The old woman was impatient. She shook the little girl's thin arm, then began to recite herself: "We will speak of the class struggle . . . every year, every month, and every day . . ."

Whereupon Ling added, in her tiny voice: "The period of socialism is a long one, and during it the danger of capitalist revisionism is ever present. . . . The most important thing is to prevent the restoration of capitalism. . . ."

As she continued to recite, Liang saw only her round mouth smeared with pancake crumbs. Her lips looked like big bruised cherries as they opened and closed, delivering the quotations from Chairman Mao, Great Leader of the proletarian class.

Liang did not fully understand these noble and venerable words, but he did not need to understand them, all he had to do was listen to them, obey them, and practice them. That was what making the Revolution meant, that was what would lead to Communism and to happiness.

"Bravo, bravo!"

Ling had completed her recitation. Grandmother Song applauded, her thin hands making a sharp sound.

"You've already learned that by heart?" Liang asked.

"Yes. Aunt Song's been coming to teach us. We all have to learn it by heart. That's what she said." The little girl put the pancake back into her mouth.

The quotations of Chairman Mao were very important; you had to have them at your fingertips. You could apply them in life only if you knew them perfectly. The school principal had told them that there was going to be a big contest of recitation from the Little Red Book. Liang now saw that if he was to become a hero, if he was to be worthy of his father, he would have to win that contest.

二十三

"Li Liang!"

"Present."

"First team."

"Yes."

Liang stepped out of the ranks and went to join the first team. He was not happy to be in that group, which was mostly incompetents. It included pupils considered too small for the second team, which would patrol the streets looking for women with long hair, symbol of the proscribed old ways. Long hair was to be forcibly cut. Assigned to the first team, also, were pupils too ignorant to belong to the third, which would search people's homes for religious objects and other relics of the old culture. And the first team included those considered deficient in courage, who were therefore ineligible for the fourth team, whose task was to climb to the top of the French church and destroy that shameful emblem of foreign domination, of the ignorance of the Chinese people, and of the nation's humiliation.

"Zhang Dashu!"

"Present!"

"Fourth team."

Liang looked at the students in his team. There were more girls than boys, and all of them, like Liang, gazed enviously at those who had been assigned to the other teams.

They set out for their posts. The first team was to go to the roads leading out of the village. There they would search people and confiscate anything that smacked of the old way or that opposed the new spirit of the Revolution.

Liang and three others, two of them girls, were sent to the east road, the most important route out of the village. It led to the town.

It was a sunny day, usual for that time of year. Liang realized they would have a lot to do, because there was little work in the fields yet, and the peasants took advantage of this to visit friends and relatives in other villages. The gifts they were taking—there might be bolts of cloth with painted patterns of no revolutionary content, or a pair of children's shoes with embroidered tiger heads, or maybe a hat for someone's grandmother that was in the old-fashioned style. Some children wore necklaces with lockets engraved with the word "Luck," an idea most certainly at odds with the spirit of the Revolution.

Liang did his work diligently, bearing most of the heavy responsibility. The two girls were hardly cut out for this task, and the other boy proved to be ignorant. "What's wrong with this thing?" he often asked. Liang would have to recite quotations from Chairman Mao to enlighten him.

The two girls acted properly only when Liang scolded them. "Our Great Leader Chairman Mao tells us . . ."

It was tiring.

"Stop, Comrade!" Liang called out sharply to a man on a loaded bicycle. A small child was perched on the handlebars, and a woman rode behind him on the rack.

"What's the matter, Comrade?" asked the cyclist warily.

"Revolutionary examination," Liang replied in a dry official tone.

The four children gathered around the family on the bicycle and began their inspection.

"Do you have a copy of the Little Red Book with you?"

asked Liang's companion. That was the only question he ever came up with.

"Yes." The man took an almost untouched copy of the Little Red Book out of his pocket. He was a young peasant and was dressed in a brand-new outfit. His bicycle was new too. He was probably on his way to his in-laws, to bring them new year's greetings.

"Don't you know you're not supposed to offer new year's greetings anymore?" Liang asked him.

"Yes," the man answered. "New year's greetings belong to the old ways, of course. We're just going to see my in-laws."

"What's this?" exclaimed one of the girls.

"Only a cake," the man replied with a humble air.

Liang noticed a red package hanging from the handlebars. He took it. "This wrapping paper is an old way. Get rid of it," he ordered in his best commander's voice.

"But it's just to make it look pretty," protested the woman, who had climbed off the back of the bicycle and taken the child in her arms.

"Look pretty. What's that supposed to mean? The prettiest thing in the world is the Revolution. That thing is an old custom. It's ugly."

The young woman was about to say something more, but her husband, who understood the situation better than she did, stopped her. He began to peel off the red wrapping paper, uncovering a box of straw-colored paper as wrinkled as an old woman's face.

Liang saw that the man and woman each wore on their chest a patch of red cloth with a quotation from Chairman Mao in yellow characters. That was in accordance with the rules. Liang carefully read the selections they had chosen, making sure they contained no mistakes and that the phrases had been properly selected to correspond accurately to the wearers. It would not be correct, for instance, for a young peasant to wear a quotation appropriate to an old man, or for a young man to wear a passage about women.

These two had chosen their quotations well. The man's read: "Never forget the class struggle." The woman's: "Struggle against selfishness and criticize revisionism." Good. Women were often selfish and ungenerous. How many brothers had had warm friendships before their marriages, only to wind up bitter enemies twenty years later, all on account of their wives? Liang liked this quotation. It reminded him of another statement by the Great Leader which, if properly understood, summed up the whole situation: "Struggle against selfishness in order to advance, criticize revisionism in order to find the right path, and we will march straight to Communism."

"Is everything all right? We're in a hurry, Comrades," the young peasant said with a smile.

Liang was about to let them go, since other people had begun to line up. But suddenly he remembered one more detail. "What's your child's name?" he asked.

"Red Rifle."

"He should be wearing a quotation on his chest too."

"Yes," the young man quickly agreed. "We tend to think of him as too little, but of course you're right. We'll have him wear a quotation too. He can learn what it means later."

He had said exactly what Liang had intended to point out, so there was nothing more to check. "All right," Liang said, "you can go."

"Wait a minute, wait a minute!" shouted Liang's companion. "Look at that!" He was pointing at the trademark on the new bicycle. It was a Flying Pigeon, one of the best-known brands in the country. "That's also old," he said.

"He's right," Liang confirmed, after giving it some thought. "You'll have to get rid of it."

"Please, comrades," the young man said, putting his big peasant hand on the trademark. "It's not my fault; it's part of the bicycle. I just bought it, and it's the first new one I've ever had."

The boy tried to pry the peasant's hand off the trademark, but the man was too strong. The boy looked to Liang for help.

Liang knew very well that even the two of them would not be able to make the man let go, so he didn't try. Then an idea came to him.

"Comrade," he said in a haughty tone, "get out your Little Red Book. We're going to study a paragraph."

The young man hesitated, but then took out his Little Red Book and opened it to the page Liang indicated.

"Read it out loud!" Liang ordered.

The young man seemed embarrassed. The little book shook in his big fingers. "I . . . don't know how to read very well," he stammered.

It seemed obvious he was telling the truth. "Then listen," Liang said, feeling very proud. "Our Great Leader Chairman Mao tells us: 'What is the best attitude to take toward a great Revolution, which closely resembles a storm? To be a revolutionary or instead to become a target of the movement?' "

The man turned pale and answered quickly, "I want to be a revolutionary."

"The Revolution wants you to take the trademark off your bicycle, because it is part of the Four Olds."

The man could think of nothing to say. He stared at the Flying Pigeon emblem.

Liang handed him a screwdriver.

After one last moment of hesitation, the man pried the plaque off sharply, as though he were tearing a demon out of his own flesh.

"Congratulations on your revolutionary act," said Liang as he took the screwdriver back.

The peasant and his family left without another word.

As the students turned to examine the next person, they heard a great commotion in the village. People were shouting, screaming, running. The other teams must have gone into action.

A young woman, her hair flying, her trousers torn, was running as fast as she could. Three boys were chasing her. "Bourgeois trousers!" they yelled.

The young woman, trying to get out of the village, ran into Liang's team.

"Stop, Comrade!" Liang ordered.

The woman stopped short and looked at him, terror in her eyes.

"Her cousin Tian Jin gave her those trousers," one of the two girls with Liang explained. "They're much too tight. Look how they cling to her thighs."

"Hold on to her!" screamed the boys who had been chasing her.

Liang reached out for the woman's wrist, but she saw him and bolted like a frightened rabbit, racing back toward the other end of the village.

"No!" Liang yelled. "This woman dares to oppose the Revolution? We can't let her get away!" He called out an order to his comrades as he joined the chase. "You stay here and guard this post. I'll catch her."

The young woman ran toward the church, with the boys in pursuit, Liang in the lead. Faster than the students, she was gaining ground.

Liang soon felt the blood pounding in his throat. He turned and looked at the others, hoping they would catch up and pass him. After all, he was not supposed to be in charge of this mission.

But the three boys were out of breath and seemed about to give up. They'd apparently decided to let Liang take care of it.

The woman ran faster, toward the church.

Suddenly a deep powerful voice boomed inside Liang's head: "The Revolution!" It was as if the woman's tight trousers were the bourgeoisie itself, a bourgeois skin that was like a fatal poison: first it would infect the woman, who was his comrade, and in time contaminate all the other comrades, and finally kill them. He had to save her, he had to protect the revolutionary arm, and that meant catching her, tearing that clothing off, and leading her back to the correct ideological path blazed by Chairman Mao. If Liang wanted to be a hero of the Revolution, if he wanted to be worthy of his father and grandfather and be a savior of the people, like all members of the Communist Party, now was the time to act, to prove his will, his faith, his courage.

A savage strength rose from the earth and flowed into his body, it propelled him like a wind, like a storm, and his legs churned madly.

The woman, exhausted, slowed down. They were at the church when Liang reached out and grabbed her by the hair. She screamed in pain.

"Stop, or I'll pull harder!"

She stopped and began to cry. "My trousers," she stammered. "My cousin Tian Jin gave them to me."

Liang felt weak. Lethargy swept through his head, through every cell of his body, loosening his fingers. He was on the verge of releasing the woman when he roused himself in alarm. No, that would ruin everything!

"A revolution is not a dinner party . . . or doing embroidery. . . . A revolution is . . . an act of violence. . . ."

The words rang in Liang's brain like troops of a revolutionary army rushing to his rescue.

The shadow that had fallen over his eyes disappeared; his fingers closed tightly; he clenched his teeth.

"Comrades, I've got her!" he shouted to the other boys, who now came up, all holding scissors.

"We will stamp out the Four Olds!" cried one of them, snapping at the woman's trousers with his scissors. The two others cut also, reducing the trousers to tatters in seconds, exposing the woman's pale thighs.

She resisted with all her strength, screaming and crying, but she didn't dare strike the boys, because they represented the revolutionary power. Finally she curled up by the wall, trying to cover her thighs with her bleeding arms.

Liang turned away as the woman wept and the boys walked off to return to their task. The sight of blood on the woman's arms and legs filled him with disgust, with shame. He never should have caught her. It was his fault that this had happened.

There was a burning in the palm of his hand—a prosecutor's hand, the hand he had used to grab the woman by the hair. It was his right hand, the one he used for writing, for playing Ping-Pong, for skipping stones on the surface of the water or hurling them into trees to drive the cicadas away. He had used that same hand to do experiments in Tian's special place. The only thing he had ever struck with that hand was doors. True, once, when his parents weren't home, he had taken a piece of pancake from Ling with that hand. . . . And now he had grabbed a woman he didn't even know by the hair because her trousers were too tight. Bourgeois trousers. He had done it for the Revolution, for the people's happiness. How could he regret it? He should be happy, because he had taken a step on the revolutionary path, on the road to heroism. No, he should not regret it. And yet he did. It was wrong to grab her by the hair. He had hurt her, and now his hand hurt too.

Absent-mindedly, Liang looked toward the church as, little by little, his body recovered its energy. It was a strange sensation.

"Hurrah!"

"Higher, higher!"

The shouts were coming from the church. Liang looked up and saw two boys halfway up the steeple, their heads visible through a window.

"Higher!" shouted a man who stood at the bottom. It was the principal.

The boys' heads disappeared. Everyone waited in silence down below. After a while, the two heads reappeared in the same window.

"It's too high. There's no way to reach it."

"It's too dangerous."

"Impossible," growled the principal, furious. He turned to the boys standing around him. "Who wants to set an example and climb to the top?" he asked.

No one answered. They all looked up at the steeple, which seemed tremendously tall.

"Who dares to climb to the top?"

Liang looked up at the steeple, which had so often filled him with awe, wonder, a sense of mystery. He scaled the pointed lead-colored monster slowly with his eyes, up to the cross at the top. The ten seemed to taunt him as it floated in a sea of clouds.

Religion, God, the Great Lord of Heaven: spiritual poison for the people, deadening their minds, miring them in ignorance in order to enslave them. Words, weighty with meaning, rushed through his mind like hammer blows, one word above all:

"REVOLUTION!"

Liang felt it explode in his heart. Trembling, he opened his mouth and cried:

"I will climb it!"

The others barely had time to turn and look at him before he had picked up an iron bar and entered the church.

二十四

Daylight was fading and the street was empty when Liang came out of the church, whose steeple was now smashed. He took a few steps on his exhausted legs, then squatted down among the rubble that testified to the day's work: broken bricks, pieces of lead, and the wooden ten. It had seemed small and fragile on top of the steeple, but on the ground it proved to be thicker than Liang's body. The crossbeam had stuck in the ground when it landed.

The wind swept up bits of paper with quotations from Mao on them. Liang and the comrades who had followed him had dropped them from the top of the church, and now they were swirling like big white butterflies in the dust. There was a roar in Liang's ears. He had never climbed so high, and his blood was still pounding.

It was getting cold, so he stood up and headed for the school. As he passed the church, he noticed that the statue of the man had been damaged. It had not been torn down, but the nose was gone, the arms had been broken, and the body was riddled with holes: Liang's comrades had been busy while he was climbing up to demolish the steeple with the iron bar. He found a piece of marble and kicked it along as he went.

When he walked through the school's gate, he stopped short. In a corner of the deserted courtyard was a mountain of objects, the result of the brilliant exploits of the third team:

a marble child with wings, some large books with gold letters, all sorts of vases, clothes of various colors, and many things he had never seen, whose names he did not know.

The Revolution had a good harvest today. With no conscious thought, Liang took a few steps toward the pile. When he looked more closely at the jumble, he recognized a smashed violin, some ripped paintings, and a few pieces of old redwood furniture with almost all the legs broken off. There were old lamps, scraps of wallpaper, and some comic books.

What an excellent job they had done! Liang felt a surge of joy, but also a pang. He was sorry he hadn't participated in this action. He was sure he would have made even more interesting discoveries. He had been good at hide-and-seek when he was little. And when his mother brought home some treat that he and his sister really liked, Wang would try to hide the leftovers, but Liang always found them.

He went over to the pile, picked up a comic book, flipped through it. The magazine was torn in three places, forming a sort of triangle ripped out of the big, colorful figure on the cover. It was an episode from the famous tale of the Three Kingdoms. The characters were dressed in old-fashioned clothes. They had big red beards and rode galloping horses as they brandished their weapons. Liang had loved reading that seemingly endless story. Reading at home, he would forget to go to school, and when he read it at school, he would forget to go home for supper. His mother stopped giving him money for comics, so he had to save up for them, or beg his friends to lend him theirs. Well, the Revolution had solved that problem: no more comics. Part of the dead past.

Liang tossed the magazine back on the pile and turned to go home. Then he noticed a rusty bucket filled with clay disks. He took out a few. They were all there: Shaved Head's famous Ape, White Face's Boat, the Young Woman with Flute, the Holy Man, the God of Longevity. There must have been a hundred of them. He began looking through them, one at a time. They had been the cause of so many quarrels, but also of so much fun. He had never been allowed to touch them. Now here they were, ruined and ownerless, tossed into a rusty bucket. What would happen to them? Probably they would be thrown into the pond, because, unlike most old objects, clay disks wouldn't burn.

"All that is old must be radically stamped out. That which can be broken will be broken. That which can be burned will be burned. That which can be neither broken nor burned will be cast into the water."

Liang stood there holding two disks, in his left hand a character he didn't recognize, an old man riding backward on a donkey, in his right Zhu-Ge Liang, a famous hero from the time of the Three Kingdoms. Liang knew him well; he had heard stories about him all his life. Suddenly he remembered the story of a particular battle. Grandfather Liu had told it to them one day when he and Tian visited the pottery workshop.

"He was a great genius," Grandfather Liu had said as he ran his potter's wheel. "It was during a war against barbarians who wore strange clothes. The imperial army had often used water to drown enemies, but these barbarians were not afraid of water. They floated easily and were very powerful. The Imperial army was on the brink of defeat when Zhu-Ge Liang arrived. 'That which does not fear water fears fire, and vice versa,' said Prime Minister Zhu. 'Fire is therefore what we need.' The barbarians, expecting an attempt to flood them out, had put on suits made of bamboo soaked in oil. These suits allowed them to float, but they burned very easily."

Liang remembered the story well, because the ending had been sad.

"As the fire roared, Zhu-Ge Liang watched from a mountaintop. There were tears in his eyes, for he knew that his life would be shortened by what he had done: he had burned men alive. And, indeed, he died very young."

"You mean he knew he was going to die young because of it, but he did it anyway?" Liang had asked.

"Of course," Grandfather Liu replied with a laugh. "He was acting in the service of his master, the Emperor Liu." There was pride in his voice, because they were of the same family.

"That which does not fear water fears fire, and vice versa."

Liang dropped the two disks back into the bucket. They shattered.

"They are old, they are poison." Liang wondered if he himself had been poisoned, because he knew many of the old stories by heart. Once again he turned to go.

But something shiny caught his eye. He could not tell what it was; he saw only a dazzling cluster of multicolored flashes. He rubbed his eyes and looked again.

He almost exclaimed aloud. They were marbles, little glass spheres with tiny flowers inside, beckoning from a bowl. Liang had long dreamed of having even a few marbles like these, not just to play with, but to look at. They were so pretty!

Cat-quick, he picked up the bowl and looked around. There was no one in the courtyard, not a sound; nothing but the smell of food coming from the neighbors' rooms.

He knew he could do it: he could take these marbles.

They were to be thrown out tomorrow anyway. He could hide them under the bed, and no one would ever know they were not lying at the bottom of the pond.

They were alluring, with those flowers inside. He had always wondered how the flowers were put in. Some were green, some yellow, some red, but they all looked like quartered oranges. "Orange marbles" was what the village children called them. Liang never had any, because his mother, a strict and serious teacher, never let him play with toys. She thought they would interfere with his schoolwork.

Liang remembered a very hot day in the town. As a reward for having done his work quickly, Wang had given him twenty fen to buy ice cream. But he had come across a peddler with a wheelbarrow full of toys.

"Toys for hair! Toys for hair!" the peddler shouted. Children who had no money would gather locks of hair and bring them to the peddler. He would check the amount of hair, then give a toy in exchange. But since Liang spent all his time studying under his mother's watchful eye, he never had a chance to go looking for hair. On that day he had watched the peddler and the other children with tears in his eyes. As he was about to walk away, a ray of light leaped through the wire mesh of the wheelbarrow and struck his heart. Riveted, he had stared at the light. Never had he felt so much pleasure, so much happiness. He was bewitched, hypnotized by the magic glimmer, as if it were turning him into a ray of light himself, pure, free of cares and sorrows.

"I want that," he had said, holding out his money.

The peddler, an honest man, had given him three marbles for his twenty fen. After admiring them for a long time—looking at them in the sun with one eye closed, feeling them with his fingers and toes, and even rolling them around in his mouth—he had hidden them in a corner of the courtyard when no one was looking, hidden them to avoid his mother's lecture about the uselessness of toys and her relentless interrogation about how he got them.

But he lost them—having hidden them too well.

Now he felt unbelievably lucky to be holding so many marbles. What ecstasy to touch them, to rub them! He dipped one finger, then two, then three, into the marbles; he felt a pleasant chill, as smooth as ice, as he wiggled his fingers in the bowl. The marbles made such a cheerful noise, as though they were laughing. . . .

The Revolution . . . Spiritual poison . . .

Liang stood as if struck by a bolt of electricity. The marbles, so lovely just a moment before, now were taunting, wicked eyes.

He felt his mind empty. Dizzy, like a sick man bedridden too long, he shook his head and took in great gulps of air as he tried to keep his balance.

"We are little heroes of the Revolution."

Sudden anger blazed in Liang's heart. He dropped the marbles, stamped on them furiously.

Deep down, he had one regret—no, two: that he had not taken the marbles, and that there had been no one in the courtyard to witness his heroism.

二十五

Wang and Ling had already eaten by the time Liang got home. When he saw the big bowl of rice and small plate of salted vegetables they had left for him, he felt his appetite return. He picked up his chopsticks, but before he had swallowed the first bite, he realized that the atmosphere in the room was strange. The heavy silence was very unusual. He turned to look at his mother and saw that she was staring at him reproachfully. He was about to ask why when his sister exclaimed, "You forgot, Liang! You forgot!"

"Oh," Liang cried, immediately putting down his chopsticks. "I'm sorry." He got up, took out his Little Red Book, and began his invocations in front of the large portrait of Chairman Mao. This was a new ritual the commune had adopted in accordance with Party directives: it was the prelude to all significant events—meals, work, classes, meetings, and before going to bed, too.

"First of all, let me wish our honorable and beloved Great Helmsman . . . unlimited and unbounded longevity . . . ten thousand years . . ."

Next came invocations to his successor, Lin Biao. Then Liang had to sing a revolutionary song.

You cannot sail the seas
* without a helmsman.*
Nothing can live without the sun. . . .

Liang put his heart into the song, but he sang off-key and in a shrill voice, which amused his little sister. At last he went back to the table.

"You remember that the contest is tomorrow?" Wang asked as he ate.

"Yes," Liang replied with his mouth full. "How could I forget something that important?"

"How much can you recite by heart?"

"About thirty paragraphs."

"Not too bad," Wang said after a moment of silence. "But to win the contest it's not enough to know a lot of quotations. You have to know some difficult passages that the others don't know. Above all, you can't make the slightest mistake. A pupil in the Zhao Zhuang school was arrested because he made an error in a quotation. The Great Helmsman said: 'We should support whatever the enemy opposes and oppose whatever the enemy supports.' But the pupil was going too fast, and he mixed up the words 'support' and 'oppose.' This was a very serious mistake, a counter-revolutionary crime. You might say it was just a slip, but how do we know he didn't do it on purpose?"

"I understand. I'll work late tonight."

"Good," said Wang. "I'll help you."

So the family spent the evening reciting from the Little Red Book, almost in chorus. Li alone was absent.

At eleven o'clock a very tired Liang decided to go to sleep. He was now used to his father's absence, knowing that new Party directives might come at any moment and that Li had to be ready to act on them at once. Liang went to bed, leaving his mother to wait up alone.

He stretched his aching limbs, which at first were reluctant to move, stiff in the cold night, but finally they warmed up and began to wriggle into crannies of his little nest. He was content. It had been a long and exciting day, especially the dizzying climb to the top of the church and the bitter taste of limestone dust under the blows of the iron bar. And then, concentrating, practicing his recitations from the Little Red Book. Now he was happy to be lying under his familiar gray blanket. Its reassuring smell soothed him. He turned over several times, thinking how good it was to be lying in the peaceful darkness in his usual place by the wall that protected the Li family from the green immensity of the fields outside. And how delightful, to be living in such a heroic, revolutionary red epoch, which would give him the chance to demonstrate his intelligence. It was like a great road leading to a mysterious future full of hope, a future in which he could become a hero, a fighter, a savior. All he had to do was continue on the path and move a little faster than the others.

Liang turned over again. Tomorrow promised to be even more exciting than today. He forced himself to close his eyes and tried to fall asleep, to make tomorrow come sooner. He saw a black screen, a swarm of momentary colored needles, a glittering, starry carpet. A little girl was sleeping in the middle. It was Wang, his mother. She woke up and was frightened. No one else was there. She began to cry.

Liang took the little girl in his arms and rocked her. He sang to her:

> *Darling, go to sleep, don't cry.*
> *Papa's gone to make the Revolution.*

He fell into a deep sleep. A boat floated in the green sea of the sorghum fields. Liang soared like a bird, flying higher and higher.

Suddenly there was a man's voice. He woke up, alarmed. But it was the voice of his father, who had come home and gone to bed.

"Are you sure that's what will happen?" Wang asked anxiously.

"Yes. I can't see any way around it. The directive just came. . . . That's why I'm so late."

Then silence filled the dark, pierced only by the reddish glow of Li's cigarette.

Wang sighed. "I don't see how it's possible," she said. "The Party has always had confidence in you. How could they do anything against you? Tell me again exactly what it said."

The reddish glow flared for a moment before Li spoke. His voice was troubled. "The aim of this movement is to overthrow those currently in power, who are taking the capitalist road. . . ."

"And?"

"And nothing. It's an order from Chairman Mao. Song wants to act on it."

"She's going to move against you?"

Complete silence.

"In any case, we have never done anything to hurt the Party."

The bird that was Liang soared again. He flew into thick black storm clouds. He turned and looked down from the steeple top, watching the printed bits of paper swirl in the wind that had just come up.

二十六

"Shit, shit, shit!"

Liang left the school building, walking as slowly as he could, each step accompanied by a muttered "Shit." Cramps tugged at his stomach; a bitter taste rose in his mouth; he snorted, dragged his feet, tripped on a stone and almost fell.

"Shit!" he said again, kicking the stone aside.

He looked around, uneasy, but no one was there. He began to walk again.

This was the first time in his life he had felt such heaviness. Guilt, fear, anger—he knew all those painful and unpleasant emotions. But, compared to this, they were more direct, easier to endure. There was a logic about them. You felt guilty because you had done something wrong; you expected to be scolded, criticized, punished. If you were afraid, terrified, you didn't dare do anything, not even move; you curled up with your hands between your thighs and waited, letting things take their course. Anger was easiest: you could throw down your bag, kick it, fly into a rage, shout, cry. Anything was better than this new feeling that offered no way to react. He felt trapped.

"Shit, shit, shit!"

He went down the alley that led to Tian's house, looking for stones as he went. He kicked aside three big ones with his right foot, three little ones with his left. The burning in his toes calmed him.

Injustice.

You had something your comrades didn't. So you showed it to them, telling them it was yours, but they took it away from you, and then they teased you, waving it under your nose and telling you that now it belonged to them, not you. No way to get it back; no one to appeal to. And if by some chance there was someone, he would take the others' side.

Liang was clenching his teeth so hard that his jaw began to hurt.

"That damn principal."

Only the other day, Liang had spoken to his father about him, explaining that he did not like the man. But his father had shaken his head, as though Liang had only himself to blame.

Well, someday Liang would be bigger than that inflated principal. Then he would punish him. He would issue all kinds of orders just to torment him. He would have him dig a well all by himself in a single day. And when the well was dug, Liang would congratulate someone else—Comrade Fang, maybe—for doing it so quickly.

At the Liu house, the black door was bolted shut, as always. He knocked and waited. The door opened with a slight creak, and he saw his friend Tian's yellowish hair.

"I'm not coming in," Liang said gruffly, tossing his head. "You come out."

Tian smiled and walked back to get something. A few seconds later he appeared with a basket on his shoulder and two pieces of sweet potato in his hand. He gave one to Liang.

They left without a word, eating the potato pieces. It was early afternoon; peasants were leading their animals out into the fields; children were going into the countryside with baskets on their shoulders.

They passed the church, which now was only a huge black hulk without a head. Or like a donkey without a tail. Two inscriptions, vertical lines of characters as big as melons, stretched across the front. Liang and Tian read them:

> *A spring wind stirs a thousand green leaves.*
> *The Empire of Heaven is filled with Good Gods.*

The first was true enough. Everywhere the leaves of weeping willows swayed in a gentle spring breeze. Spring had arrived late, after much turmoil, much anticipation. Someone had said it was like an opera singer who deliberately makes the audience wait. The violins would screech and the drums would rumble, while the singer stood in the wings.

But spring was here now. The sun leaned closer over the roofs. Willows and poplars cast their flowers, which floated through the air like snow. Insects, awakening after their long slumber, came to life. Swarming together, they swirled in a frenzy, parading their existence.

Liang, walking beside Tian, put the last piece of potato in his mouth. As he chewed, his friend mumbled: "Filled with Good Gods . . ."

It was true: both of the Great Helmsman's lines had come to pass. Everyone in this spring-filled land now acted like a god, even the comrade who guarded the melon field. Little Red Books in hand, Chairman Mao medallions pinned to their chests, red armbands in place: the Red Guards.

"The Cultural Revolution . . ."

"To rebel is justified."

"Let us seize power from those who now wield it."

Everyone walked resolutely, like soldiers, arms swinging, backs stiff, speaking only to say: "Chairman Mao tells us . . ." That was always the phrase, even when you were planting wheat or scolding an animal that had stepped out of its furrow.

"You were the best. There's no doubt about that," said Tian in the tone of one who would allow no other opinion.

They left the village and headed toward Dry River, to where the silk leaves grew, a place Tian knew well. Liang cast a grateful glance at his friend.

Tian was dragging his feet as he walked, deliberately stirring up dust. "That little girl—what's her name? Yellow Flower—made a lot of mistakes. Even I noticed it. Instead of saying 'the masses of the people' she said 'the people of the masses'!"

Liang answered his friend by dragging his feet too. The dust behind them swirled high under the blazing sun, like a dragon's long yellow tail.

"They congratulated her and not you, but you were the best. Believe me, no one ever recited that passage you used in the contest."

"Shit!" Liang shouted. Then he put his hand over his mouth.

"Don't worry. I won't tell anyone."

They reached the bank of the river, a dry slash in the yellow earth. There was water only during the rainy season, when torrents came and often flooded the village, turning the fields into swamps. Castor-oil bushes had been planted between two little ridges.

As part of the Cultural Revolution, Chairman Mao had ordered children to participate in the work of the peasants. The school had decided to raise silkworms as its project, and the pupils had to go into the fields every day to pick leaves to feed the worms. Liang and Tian had found this spot to be rich in good leaves, and they came here every afternoon.

They worked quickly, and soon the basket was almost full, so they lay down to rest. Light clouds, almost transparent, drifted above them. The sun seemed to purr like a dozing cat.

"Why don't you write a dazibao denouncing the principal?" asked Tian. "He wasn't fair in that contest."

"Me? I should make a poster saying that *I* was the best? That's stupid!"

Tian thought about it. "Oh, of course, you can't be the one to do it. I'd do it for you, except I don't know how to write."

The boys rolled over on their backs and closed their eyes against the sun. Suddenly Liang thought of something. He looked frantically around them.

"What are you looking for?" Tian asked, trying to follow his friend's glance.

"Do you remember that day in the fields when we heard the strange sound? The thing you said was the cry of the Wen Meng?"

Tian turned pale. "You never forget anything, do you?" he mumbled. "My grandfather died . . ."

He did not finish. Liang continued to look around, as if driven by some force outside himself.

"That cry . . . I never heard it again after that."

He stood up, looked everywhere, in vain.

"And you won't hear it again," Tian said with tears in his eyes.

"Why won't he cry out anymore?" Liang complained. "It was such a pretty sound." He sat down again, and a moment later the boys were picking more leaves.

"There must be something we can do against that principal," Tian said as he flattened the leaves in the basket.

"I don't see how. He's in charge. He has the power."

"That's it! Didn't Chairman Mao say we should overthrow those who hold power? We're supposed to rebel!"

Tian was right! Liang's face flushed. How often had he told himself that he wanted to become a hero of the Revolution, that he must always be the first to execute the Great Helmsman's orders? How could it have taken him so long to understand this situation?

A revolution is not a dinner party or doing embroidery. . . . A revolution is an act of violence by which one class overthrows another.

"Let's go!" Liang picked up the basket without waiting for his friend. He was filled with intense revolutionary energy. "Let's go back and write some dazibaos!"

二十七

The basket of leaves had never felt so light. He had never walked so fast. It was as if his legs were flying ahead on their own. Tian had to run so he wouldn't lose sight of his friend in the whirlwind of dust they were raising.

They delivered the leaves to the teacher in charge of the silkworm project and asked for some paper and ink.

"Why?" asked the teacher, looking strangely at Liang.

"To write dazibaos, of course."

The teacher stood woodenly, not reacting.

"We want to write . . . like the others," said Tian, who was standing behind Liang.

"Like the others," the teacher murmured, staring at them. "I guess you haven't heard."

He finally went to the office to look for paper. About five minutes later, he came back and told the boys there was no paper. "Your comrades took all of it," he explained.

"When can we get some?" Liang persisted. "We have important things to write."

"It's for the Revolution," Tian said softly.

"How about tomorrow?" Liang asked.

"Tomorrow . . . Yes, by tomorrow I guess you'll know all about it," the teacher said, looking up, not at them.

The boys, disappointed, decided to try again the next day. They said good-bye.

It was twenty-six and a half big steps or thirty-five small ones across the courtyard;

Liang had counted them often enough. Today he took big steps, driven by his revolutionary spirit and by the anticipated pleasure of telling his mother about his plan.

But, though he had practiced what he would say, he found himself unable to speak when he reached their room. Instead, he stopped, dumbfounded, like a puppet whose strings had been cut. A strange smell made him take a step backward. He tried not to cough.

"Don't say a thing," Wang ordered.

"What is it? What's that smell?" The questions tumbled out against his will.

"Just don't say a thing!"

His mother's voice was like a cold shower, an icy gust of wind.

Wang was trembling. Tearing her frightened eyes from Liang's, she mumbled, "It's nothing . . . I've done nothing."

Liang dashed past her. A few fragments of glazed paper lay smoking in a little pile of gray ashes behind the door.

"Grandfather's picture!"

"Hold your tongue!" shouted Wang. She pushed him aside and put her foot on the ashes.

"But that was the only picture of him! You gave it to me!"

Wang stared at him, as though she hadn't heard.

"Mama, why did you burn it?"

Still she said nothing.

"It was your father," Liang whispered, "my grandfather . . . the only photograph."

To Liang it was like a terrible bloodletting. Something vital and precious inside him had left with that smoke, making him weak.

Wang, now calm, smoothed a lock of Liang's hair and

took him by the hand. They sat on the big bed. She looked deep into her child's eyes.

"Mama . . ." Liang said faintly.

"It's too complicated to explain," she said. "But remember one thing: Don't ever say another word about that photograph. I want to forget your grandfather."

"Forget my grandfather?"

"If anyone asks, say you never saw his photograph, that I never told you anything about him. All right?"

Liang looked at his mother. She looked back. It was a wordless exchange: urgent questions withheld, painful explanations not given.

Liang nodded, very slowly.

"Yes, Mama."

His mother's expression was hidden in the darkness. Liang could read no approval in it, but he felt her squeeze his hand a little tighter.

"We'll eat supper as soon as Ling gets home."

Liang looked out the window. He could feel the blackness of the night, thick, velvety, capable of healing heartbreak or wounds of the flesh. Could it also fill the abyss of despair?

There was a knock at the door. "Is Professor Wang there?"

"What is it?" Wang answered, her voice calm.

"I am from the local committee of the Cultural Revolution. I have been instructed to inform you that Li will not be coming home tonight."

Liang felt a pang when he heard the man say "Li." He had never before heard his father's name pronounced with such insolence.

"Why not?" he shouted.

The man did not answer, but left as suddenly as he had come.

Liang was about to run after him, but his mother would not let go of his hand. She gripped it tighter.

"So . . . it has begun."

Suddenly she started crying, in front of Liang.

二十八

It was night. Liang closed his eyes and waited. He knew that his father would not be coming home, but he also knew that he would not be able to fall asleep, still waiting.

His mother had turned over twice, but now she had stopped moving. Was she asleep? Liang thought not. She was probably listening to him. Tonight she would not scold him if he fidgeted, but it would be better if he didn't fidget. His restlessness would only make hers worse.

Night reigned outside, but Liang noticed that the silence was not complete; there were noises, sometimes loud ones. The more you tried to bury your head, the more clearly you heard them. Shouts reached your ears, and you saw images that shifted. If you looked at them hard enough, you could pick out shapes. A big tree. You were stripping the bark, and soon you could see its white skin underneath, moist with greenish sap. You peeled off more bark. A piece of the tree fell off, but you kept on peeling, deeper and deeper. Keep going, show no mercy! Finally the hole goes all the way through. But don't give up! . . . Then the tree reappears, with the moon. In the moon is a rabbit named Wukeng, who has been ordered to cut down the tree. But with each swing of the ax, the tree closes up as though it has never been struck, so the rabbit must keep chopping forever. . . . It was Grandfather Liu who told him the story about the rabbit and the tree. Tian's grandfather, not his. His own grandfather had died during the Long March. Or had he? Liang wasn't sure anymore. Had he died for the Revolution, a hero of the Party, as Liang had thought? Now he didn't know. Why had his mother burned the photograph, and acted so strangely? Unless . . . Lord of Heaven! Liang could not imagine what would happen then. It would be bad.

The night shifted impatiently above the house as though waiting for the spring holiday. Its enormous bulk blocked the next day's path. Yet it was the next day that Liang wanted. Then he would find out what had happened to his father, and what it was that had begun. That's what his mother had said: "It has begun."

He awoke to great commotion in the courtyard. When he turned to ask his mother what it was, he saw that she was not in the room. Nor was his sister. There was no time to think. He got up and dressed.

"Let's go! Get the dazibaos in the street first!"

"But we need fifty people for the red flags."

"Who's going to lead the chants?"

Liang went out without eating.

At school there was chaos. No one was in class. The pupils were forming into lines. Some carried flags; others, dazibaos.

"Li Liang! Get in line, right now!" his teacher shouted.

The minute he had taken his place beside Tian, the group moved into the street and began marching toward the village center. Liang walked mechanically, hearing the flapping of the flags being waved back and forth and the tramping of what seemed like thousands of people through a sea of dust.

A platform had been set up in front of the former church.

Nearly all the district's inhabitants were lining up carefully around it, like a solemn army. They were dressed alike: the men in black, their hair cropped short; the women in blue, their hair cut straight across the back of the neck. Everyone sported the largest possible Chairman Mao button, and they wore red armbands.

Some began pasting dazibaos on the walls and handing out printed leaflets. Liang took one and read:

"Mass rally of the commune to overthrow Li Xian Yang and Zhao Jialu, the holders of capitalist power. Their crimes . . ."

Thunder clapped in Liang's head. All the pupils around him had read the leaflet too, and they were looking at him with wolves' eyes. Some began to laugh; others whispered. Tian, his head bowed and his fists clenched, stood motionless beside Liang.

Someone called the rally to order. The crowd pressed closer around the platform as Song mounted it with a loud yell. A tight belt around her waist made her look thinner, but Liang saw only the whites of her eyes and the red Mao medallion on her chest. With a crisp gesture she took out her Little Red Book and waved it in front of the large portrait of Chairman Mao in the center of the platform. She recited her invocations to the Great Helmsman.

Finally she turned back to the crowd and began to speak: "Our Great Helmsman tells us: 'Who owns the sky? We do. Who owns the land? We do. It is therefore up to us to speak and to act.' "

Glaring fiercely, she rolled her sleeves up to her elbows, reached into her shirt and took out a crumpled piece of paper, and began to read:

"Li Xian Yang is the greatest holder of capitalist power in our commune. He has relentlessly led us down the capitalist road ever since his arrival here. To begin with, he has constantly sought to demean the Revolution through his obsession with production. He harps on grain output and makes us dig wells endlessly, but deviously he conceals his real aim, which is to prevent us from doing the most important thing: making the Revolution. Again and again I suggested to him that we strive systematically to root out and destroy religion, but on each occasion he diverted me from that goal. Think about it, comrades! We made the Revolution to overthrow the bourgeois class: a surplus of production, a new prosperity, will only bring forth the detestable bourgeoisie all over again!"

Song stopped to swallow and catch her breath. Pleasure and anger were mingled in her expression. Fingering her piece of paper, she transferred it to the other hand and continued:

"It is time to wake up! To see things clearly! A man such as this, a traitor to our ideals, can only lead us back to the terrible conditions that prevailed before the Revolution! I ask you now, dear comrades, to allow me to bring this renegade before you."

Dust rose as the crowd stirred. A tall young man leaped to the platform, raised his right fist, and shouted:

"Down with Li Xian Yang!"

"Overthrow the regime that is leading us back to capitalism!

"Crush the filthy dog who would bring back capitalist misery!

"Long live the revolutionary line of Chairman Mao."

The crowd greeted each phrase with a thunderous howl. Liang, barely daring to raise his head, watched as his father, bent forward, wrists held behind his back by two strong men, was dragged onto the platform and thrown to his knees. Liang's heart was rocked by hammer blows. Shame burned his body and struck his face, and he staggered with dizziness.

Suddenly he heard something. In the midst of the whirlwind of shouting, the rhythmic noise of stamping feet, he heard a soft sound, a sigh that seemed meant for him alone, a consoling whisper in his ear.

When he turned to look, he saw only a forest of raised arms rhythmically pumping to the shouts of revolutionary slogans.

At the same time, something small crept slowly and timidly into the hollow of his left hand. He closed his fingers on it, grasping at that tenderness as a starving man grasps at bread. There was another sigh. Tian had given him his hand. Liang held it tight, but did not dare look at his friend. He no longer had the right.

Song's voice came again from the platform: "Look! Here is the man who wants to lead us back to the kind of society we have condemned. Here is the loathsome tongue that issues contemptible orders! Here is the head that instills foul ideas!"

"Down with the renegade!"

"May Li Xian Yang be cast down forever! May he be crushed and never rise again!"

More shouts.

"And here is even more telling evidence: wherever he goes, Li Xian Yang always uses his capitalist authority to find someone to serve as his slave. My own mother became his victim. My mother, dear comrades, an old woman over sixty, has been forced to work from dawn to midnight every day taking care of Li's bourgeois daughter!"

Song's voice was choked with sobs.

"Avenge Grandmother Song!"

"May the debt of blood be paid in blood!"

There was a sharp crack. Song had slapped Li's left cheek. Then she burst into tears.

The melon guard jumped up to the platform. His speech was cruder, a mixture of insults and revolutionary slogans. He sprayed spit on the paper he was holding, but he never looked at it, since he couldn't read.

He denounced all those in power: Li, for sacrificing a prime piece of land under the pretext of digging an irrigation ditch; Zhao Jialu, for having been too cowardly to oppose Li; the school principal, for having excessively criticized the pupils, who were now little revolutionary generals; the man in charge of the grain warehouse; the storekeeper; the caretaker at the commune office, who had twice refused to let him in.

All the people he named were led onto the platform, amid new shouts. Among them was Liu, Tian's father, who was accused of being the ringleader of the religious movement in the village and of being Li's accomplice in his agricultural reforms.

Red Guards from other villages took over to denounce their leaders, who were also dragged onto the platform. Finally, a committee was elected to direct the Cultural Revolution in each commune. Song and the melon guard were put in charge of Liang's village. It was decided to lock the renegades up so that they would be unable "to speak and act wrongly and misguidedly" and in order to prevent them from "using their influence on the masses to destroy the movement."

The rally went on until late in the afternoon.

二十九

Cold enveloped Liang. It was night. The shouting had stopped. The printed leaflets, scattered in the silence of the deserted square, caught the glimmer of the red-tinged crescent moon. As the wind swept the leaflets away, the village sank deeper into darkness.

"Liang . . . shouldn't we go home?"

Tian's fingers moved in Liang's hand. This roused Liang from the refuge deep inside himself where he had been hiding all day.

"Well," said Tian, climbing to his feet, "I'm going home." He tugged at Liang. Liang was confused at first, but slowly stood up, tottering. He gripped Tian's hand like a shipwrecked sailor clinging to a lifeline and walked beside him in silence. The shouts of the crowd still haunted him. Phrases still burned, like flames inside demented clouds:

"Li Xian Yang is a renegade." "Everything he did was anti-Party." "He was deceiving the Party all along." "Liang, his son, shows his claws against the Revolution."

Liang wished he could trample those clouds underfoot. He tried to crush them with each step, or at least make them change their course. Finally he managed it. The clouds rolled back. The hateful messages vanished, and others took their place: "It's not true. . . . An injustice has been done to Li Xian Yang. . . . Song went much too far. . . . What happened today is no more than a passing ordeal for my father—for my father and for me."

"We're here," murmured Tian. He tried to withdraw his hand from his friend's.

Liang looked up and saw the black door in front of him. He let go of Tian's hand, but his own remained cupped; that gave him the comforting feeling that they were still holding hands.

"I'm going in," said Tian, pushing the heavy door open. "What about you? Don't you want to go home?"

"Yes. I guess so. . . . My mother . . ."

Tian's frail back disappeared into the courtyard, and the black door closed. Liang started for home, alone. The street was deserted. The village families, confused by the day's upheavals, had curled up in their houses like snails, gathering on the wide beds of hard-packed earth heated by the evening meal's fire. Men smoked their pipes. Women did chores. They talked about the day's events in casual tones, but they were all alert for any commotion in the street, ready to rush out at a moment's notice to contribute whatever "testimony" might be required. Any tale, however ridiculous, could be built up and built up if it was repeated often enough.

Liang listened to his footsteps echoing off the walls of the alley. He had walked this way so often, whenever he went to see his friend, but somehow he had never noticed that on one side the blackened bricks, scored by years of wind, rain, and sun, smiled out of strange and ugly faces; on the other, the walls of hard-packed earth, older than the bricks, slouched with a weary yellow look. The alley seemed shorter than usual, but not as narrow. He wished it were one of those tiny twisting ones that only one person at a time could fit through. He wished it was darker, colder, that the ground was sandy and hard to walk on. Then he could go slower, bent over, with his eyes closed. He would feel protected, walking on a path no reasonable person would think to try.

Liang saw that he was almost at the end. He counted his steps: one, two, three. He wiped his nose with his sleeve, wiped the sleeve on his pants. One more step, and he would be out. He would turn right along the pond and go through the school's gate; then he would see the lighted window of their room. He would push the door open, cross the threshold. . . . And then?

"Please don't let me run into anyone on the way. Please don't let anyone see me go in."

When he reached the far corner of the courtyard, he stopped to catch his breath. He breathed as quietly as possible. Now he had to take the last steps. He could think of no way to make the walk home last any longer. He had to go in, like a wounded dog. You always return, instinctively, he thought, even when you know that the house has collapsed, that the family has been shattered, that the master of the house is not there anymore to protect you.

A door creaked. Someone was coming. No time to think anymore. He took a step, saw the window. To his surprise, it was dark. There was no sign of life. He walked faster, reached the door and pushed it open. Entering the darkness, he went to light the lamp.

"No! No light!"

His mother's husky voice came from the far corner of the room.

"All right," Liang said quietly, as if nothing had happened. "Isn't Ling home yet?"

There was no response.

"I'll go look for her," he said, happy to have an excuse to leave.

"No, I'm here!" Ling blurted from another corner. She was crying.

Liang felt the ground tilt under him as he listened to the grief in the stifling blackness of the room. He wanted to cry out. By howling like a wolf he could free himself from this engulfing despair. The cry was there in his throat; he had only to loosen his grip and it would come forth.

Ling's tears subsided but didn't stop. It was always like that when she didn't get something she wanted. She would sob on and on, like a machine.

Liang's need to howl began to ease its grip on his throat. He took a few steps, reached the bed, sat down. His head slumped and his eyes closed. The seconds ticked away.

Women are flesh, but men are bones, so it's our job to hold the women up. Liang had not forgotten Grandfather Liu's deep, rough voice telling him this. Everything the old man said had been mixed with the rumble of phlegm that he never managed to clear out of his throat.

Liang was a man, though ten years old. So he too was bone. Now he had to play his proper role. He moved his right arm to reassure himself that his bone really existed and to remind himself how bone felt: hard, strong.

"If you're hungry, there's some corn bread in the basket," Wang said from her corner.

"No, thanks," Liang replied in a brighter tone. He raised his head and groped for words. "You know, Mama. I've always thought that it feels warmer in the dark than with the light on."

No response. Except for Ling's weeping, which now sounded like a sorrowful gurgle.

"Mama? Last night I dreamed that my friends back in town wanted me to enter a Ping-Pong tournament. I was a good player, remember? But I never liked tournaments. . . . Now I don't even know how to play anymore, since they don't have any tables here."

"So you didn't play?" little Ling asked, curious. She had stopped gurgling.

"I don't know. It was only a dream."

"What's a dream?"

"What! You don't know what a dream is?"

"No, what is it?"

"I saw you having one just the other day. You were moving your lips while you were asleep, as if you were eating pancakes that Grandmother . . ." Liang broke off, annoyed at himself for having brought that subject up. "Anyway," he said, "you were dreaming."

"Why didn't you tell me the next day?"

"I forgot," he said. His tone changed when he asked: "Mama, do you want me to light the fire and make some corn mush for her? She must be hungry. She's only a child."

"No. I can go to bed without eating too!" the little girl hollered.

"All right, let's see who'll be first to say, 'I'm starved.' "

"All right!" Ling answered triumphantly.

The children lay down side by side in the darkness, without undressing and without getting under their blankets.

Silence covered everything, making the darkness even darker.

Liang opened his eyes. It was going to be another beautiful day. The first glimmer of light trickled through the small window. The sun looked like the yolk of a soft-boiled egg slightly flattened and about to run. Liang watched the shimmering as it crept up the dirty windowpane. Layers of dust shaped like rugged mountains and sharp ridges appeared in the path traced by the reddish glow. That worried Liang: the ridges might crack the yellow egg. He closed his mouth, held his breath. But the light was moving up the window too slowly to keep the egg safe by holding his breath. He gave up, breathed again.

"Mama!" Ling was awake already.

"What?" answered Wang, who was preparing breakfast.

"I'm not going to Grandmother Song's today, am I?"

"Certainly not."

"Where am I going, then?"

"You're staying home," said Wang after a moment's thought.

"All right. But I left my red barrette there," the little girl complained.

Liang opened his eyes wide. He heard someone knocking at the door.

"Professor Wang," a voice said, "would you come outside for a moment?"

Liang sat up in bed and watched his mother go out. He and his sister tried to hear what was being said, but the voices were too faint. They got only snatches.

"Liang, what does 'criticize' mean? And 'traitor'?"

"Be quiet!" Liang growled. He had heard nothing more than "We'll see you in a little while."

Wang was very pale when she came back into the room. She continued making breakfast without a word.

"What is it?" Liang asked in a grown-up voice, as though he had the right to know about things that would affect him.

Wang glanced at him. "Nothing," she muttered, barely moving her lips. "Both of you, get up. And listen: I don't want you to leave the room today. I have a meeting in a little while, and I have to write a report."

She finished making breakfast and put it on the table. Without eating, she sat down at a corner of the trunk she used as a desk.

Liang waited, not sure what to do. But when Ling, who never managed to button her clothes properly, got up, he did too, to help her get dressed.

"You didn't do it right either," she whined, pointing to a button out of place.

Liang was paying no attention to her. He glanced over at his mother, curious to see what she was writing. As if she had eyes in the back of her head, she turned so he could not look over her shoulder.

The children, dressed and washed, sat down at the table. Liang watched his mother. She would sit motionless for a moment, looking thoughtful; then there would be a rustling sound as she wrote a few lines and immediately crossed them out. Then she would sit and think, write a few more lines, and cross them out. She pushed some pages aside, which Liang thought she meant to throw away.

"Mama," he said, "if you don't hurry up, the mush will get cold."

"I'm coming," his mother answered.

Liang was encouraged by her quiet tone. "What are you writing?" he asked.

Wang turned toward him. Liang gasped. His mother's face was blood-red; her eyes were flashing, her lips trembling. He had never seen her so upset. It was as if she were not his mother.

"Mama!" Liang cried sharply, as if to pull her back from the edge of an abyss, to cut the invisible hooks that were dragging her into a terrible fire.

"Mama, Mama!" Ling also called, tears in her eyes.

Wang buried her face in her hands and turned to the wall without a word.

The children, frightened, fell silent, unable to take their eyes off their mother. She finally dropped her hands from her face and sat staring vacantly at the wall.

After a very long silence, she brushed a lock of her hair back with her right hand.

This homey maternal gesture lifted the stone from Liang's heart. "Mama," he said softly, "you have to eat."

"Yes, I will," said Wang, her voice normal now.

She sat down at the low table and took a few mouthfuls from her bowl.

"Listen carefully," she said to the children. "I don't want you to leave this room today. No matter what. Do you hear?"

Liang nodded obediently.

"What if I have to pee?" asked Ling. There was no toilet in the room. They had to go outside the courtyard.

"You can't," Wang ordered.

The little girl didn't dare say anything more.

After quickly finishing her breakfast, Wang threw open the big trunk, took out all the summer clothes, and put the winter ones away. Then, apparently deciding that it might still get cold, she took the winter clothes out again and put the summer ones back. She did this two or three more times. Next she began a determined, careful search of the room. Chasing the children from one corner to another, she crouched down to look under the big bed, stood on a stool to reach the top of the window frame. She emptied drawers, flipped through the books, and felt along the sheets, the blankets, and even the dusty little curtain, which had not been touched since they hung it at the window on the day they arrived. In no time, Wang had turned the entire room upside down. It looked like a nest where chickens had just hatched.

"What are you trying to find, Mama?" Liang asked, relieved that he had not hidden any clay disks, comic books, or marbles in the room.

"Nothing," Wang said. "Move over."

As she was going through the box that held their shoes, there were noises in the courtyard, the sound of footsteps approaching.

"Will you come with us, Comrade Wang?" a man outside said in a threatening voice.

Wang picked up some of the crumpled pieces of paper and left without a word, her legs unsteady.

There was silence in the little room. Ling, after a while, began to pick up a few of the scattered objects, humming to herself as she found some ribbons for her hair. Liang noticed a few things he had hidden under the bed and then forgotten: an earthenware bowl that Grandfather Liu had given him, a rusty knife, a little green bottle. He looked at these objects, which lay in a heap as if waiting for their former owners to come and reclaim them. An inner voice urged him to get up and do something. The knife was rusty, but it still cut pretty well, and the bowl looked nice. He was about to help his sister, who was busy trying to put on one of her old shoes, when he heard shouts coming from a classroom.

"Make the traitor's daughter stop lying!"

"Make her say what is hidden in her heart!"

Liang turned quickly toward the door and grabbed the knob.

"Liang!" Ling said faintly, her left foot halfway into the shoe. "Mama said we can't go out today."

Liang let go of the knob. Standing at the door, he listened, but heard nothing else. Then he had an idea. He went to the big trunk and found a few pages Wang had written but left behind.

"I never saw my father," he read. "He left with the army when I was barely three months old. I therefore have no way of knowing what he did in the army. I never heard from him after the Liberation, nor did I ever hear anything about him."

But that's not true, Liang thought. What about the photograph? He turned to another page.

"I was born to a family of wealthy landlords, a family of the exploiting class. Although I never saw my father or mother, or my grandfather, who formerly was the lord of the region, I can well imagine the ugly faces of those who lived by exploiting the people. Today, thanks to the revolutionary masses, I have come to realize, deep down, that though I was raised by the Communist Party and grew up in the new society, I was born of the flesh and blood of the exploiters. . . ."

Liang began to tremble as he read. He held his breath and turned to the third page.

"As a child of exploiters, and having neglected the

opportunity for reeducation held out to me by the revolutionary masses, I was unable to become a member of the great family of the Revolution and therefore was unable to exert a positive influence on my husband's work. . . ."

All the pages had many corrections.

Liang was baffled. He could not imagine how his mother, a devoted revolutionary, could have written such things. He recalled her words, her actions—none of them had been like this. He read it a second time. He was devastated.

"Only to a general's family can a general be born." "Your grandfather was a hero of the Eighth Route Army." "Don't ever say a word about that photograph . . . forget your grandfather." "Your grandfather and his comrades founded a new society." "The ugly faces of those who lived by exploiting the people." "Born to a family of the exploiting class."

All this churned in Liang's head. He fell onto the bed, scattering the pages.

"What's this writing?" asked Ling, picking up a page and pretending to read.

"Nothing," said Liang, biting his lip. "Just a report."

Ling looked at her brother with soft shining eyes, as if wanting to believe him. She fingered the pages and read the few words she'd learned in the nursery school in the town: "I . . . he . . . you." She began to fold a page. "I'll make a boat out of it," she said.

He heard shouts again.

"The only way out is total surrender!"

"Leniency for those who unburden their hearts completely!"

"Severe punishment for those who hold out against the Revolution!"

Liang could not stand it. He circled the room three times, then ran to the door.

"Liang!" his sister called.

He threw the door open and ran toward the classroom across the courtyard. Through the window he saw many heads, both men and women, like a black wave. He hoisted himself up and peered through the glass. His mother was standing in the middle of the crowd. Head down, she was talking in a broken voice.

"Please believe me, dear comrades. I have no way of knowing what my father did in the Red Army. I was too young. . . ."

"Lies!" a voice barked. "How can you expect us to believe that a daughter is ignorant of the life her father leads?"

Wang hesitated. "But it's true," she answered. "I don't know anything about him. Whenever I asked a question about my father, my grandmother, who raised me, would always say the same thing: 'He went to fight the Japanese invaders; he's a general in the Red Army now.' And I believed her."

A man yelled: "A landlord's son, a repulsive intellectual, an exploiter, could only be an enemy of the Red Army. You are lying!"

Wang said nothing. A young woman Liang knew from school grabbed his mother by the hair, shook her violently, and hurled accusations: "Wang Chu Hua, I'm telling you: Stop trying to hide the truth! We are soldiers armed with Mao Zedong Thought. Our eyes are as clear as snow water. Your grandfather was the biggest landlord in the district, a man who exploited the peasants to their death. Your father pretended to aid the Revolution, but in fact he tried to make the Red Army lose. As for you, you were hidden like a time bomb next to the Party leadership. What influence did you have on Li Xian Yang's counterrevolutionary acts? What conspiracy did you pass down from your ancestors? If you want mercy, you must tell us everything that is buried in your heart. . . ."

Liang felt a knife in his own heart.

"What are they doing in there, Liang?" Ling asked in her tiny voice. She took her brother's hand and tried to boost herself up to see. Liang looked at her dirty little hand. He could think of nothing to say.

"Is Mama in there?"

"No!" Liang said fiercely, feeling like a wounded wild animal. "What are you doing out here anyway?"

"I . . . I have to pee."

She began to cry.

"Go away!" Liang shouted. He pulled his hand from his sister's and ran toward the fields.

He wanted to run for hundreds, thousands of kilometers, to cross the fields of corn and sorghum, scale the mountains, swim the seas, and leave this world behind him, leave it for another world, whether hell or paradise.

He ran until he came to the soundless hidden place where no one lived and nothing grew except a few shoots of yellow grass, thin and frail. He threw himself like a rabbit onto the soil, as if plunging into a sea turned solid. He beat the ground with his fists, feet, elbows, even his head.

Finally, exhausted, he rolled over and abandoned his limbs, his whole body, even his soul, to the eternal dusty yellow earth, whose broad, solid chest had borne all his blows and all his insults. The earth warmed him, soothed his wounds, absorbed his rage.

Lying there, his face to the sun, Liang breathed deeply through his mouth. He listened to the silence. Time seemed to stand still, as if the seconds were piling up behind him and would soon drown him. He should turn over and let them pass; maybe they would carry away some of his hatred. But his limbs refused to move.

The seconds became minutes, the minutes hours, submerging him in a flood of time. He fought against it, he gasped for air, mouth wide open, sucking in time and blowing it out in great puffs.

The sun, driven by his labored breathing,

slowly detached itself from the clouds and began the second, more arduous half of its journey.

What if he were someone else? Suppose Li Xian Yang were not his father, or Wang Chu Hua his mother. Where would he be now? What kind of life would he be leading? Suppose his mother had been born to a poor family. Suppose his grandfather had not died in the Revolution, and Wang had married another man, someone who never became a prefect. What would Liang be then? What would have become of him? He would not even be named Li Liang. He would have a different body, half what he was now, half someone else. Funny to think about being half of yourself. Maybe he could share Tian's body, or Zhang Dashu's. He would have yellowish hair and a flattened nose that constantly sniffled streams of snot. But at least he would be at peace. He would watch this revolutionary turmoil from a distance, casually, hands in his pockets. He might even play with Shaved Head or White Face and make fun of that kid Li Liang, who wanted to be a future general, a hero of the Revolution, but in fact was nothing but a child of bad birth, the fruit of a plot against the Communist Party.

But that wasn't true! Or was it?

Preposterous ideas rattled in Liang's head, colliding into one another and forming ideas even more preposterous, until finally he had no ideas at all. He was an empty shell, a skull without a brain. His limbs had no flesh, his eyes no pupils. But his stomach rumbled: he was hungry.

He turned and looked at the wheat swaying in the breeze. Smiling and respectful, the stalks leaned their thousand heads toward him as if begging him not to eat them. He sneered, tore off a handful of wheat, put it in his mouth, chewed with hatred.

He heard a voice. "Liang! Liang!" It was Tian. "Liang, I'm over here."

Liang looked at him without a word, still chewing the wheat.

"Look, I brought you a sweet potato," Tian said, holding up something wrapped in a dirty rag. He didn't dare come closer. Liang spat out the half-chewed wheat and looked silently at the package.

"Here." Tian waved it, keeping his distance.

"Give it to me," Liang finally said. He lay back, feeling giddy.

Tian ran over, knelt beside him, and unwrapped the rag. Liang took the sweet potato.

"Grandmother asked me to bring it to you."

Liang said nothing. He finished the potato in just a few bites.

Tian looked at him. "Are you going to go back?"

"No. I'm not going home."

"Do you want to come to my house?"

"No," Liang said, looking up at the sun.

"Should we stay out here until it gets dark?" Tian asked, sitting on the ground. He too looked up at the sun. "Do you want me to tell you a story, Liang?" he asked after a while.

"If you want . . ."

Tian tucked his legs under him. Swaying like an old man, he began:

"There's a pile of gold where the sun sets. That's why sunsets blaze. Once upon a time, there were two brothers who lived in the west. The older one was very rich, because he had inherited the best land. All he gave his little brother was a small patch of land that produced almost nothing, no matter how hard the young man worked.

"One year, the two brothers sowed their fields as usual. The older one planted corn, which always gave him a good harvest, but the younger brother's soil was so bad that the only thing he could plant was sorghum, which grows even in the desert. But when autumn came, his field had only one sorghum, very large and very red, its kernels almost the size of soybeans.

"Every day, the young man went out into his field to look at his sorghum plant, waiting impatiently for the time to pick the grain. But the day before harvest time, the kernels disappeared. The younger brother was so sad, he cried for three days.

"He cried so hard, the eagle who had eaten the sorghum felt guilty. The eagle went to the young man and said: 'It was I who ate your sorghum, because it was so pretty.'

" 'Yes, it was pretty,' the younger brother said to the eagle. 'But couldn't you see that it was the only one in the field, my own harvest for the entire year? Now I have no food.'

"The eagle was surprised. He asked the young man why he was so poor. The young man told the eagle about his older brother. The eagle became very angry and decided to help the young man.

" 'Do you see where the sun sets?' he asked. 'There's much gold and treasure there. Climb on my back, and I'll take you there. But you will have only a little time. We must leave before the sun reaches its nest; otherwise we'll be burned to death.'

"The young man climbed on, and at dawn the eagle flew off. They arrived just before sunset. The young man saw a mountain of gold nuggets. He reached down and picked only one nugget. The eagle asked him why he took so little.

" 'It's enough for me,' the young man said.

"He returned to the village, and with his gold bought a lot of grain and a good piece of land. And he lived happily ever after.

"The older brother was surprised at his brother's new prosperity. He asked him where his money came from. The young man, who was very trusting, told him the story of the eagle. The following year, the older brother, instead of sowing corn in his good fields, planted sorghum. But the sorghum grew abundantly. So he cut down all his plants but one and that one was huge and loaded with kernels. Every day he went out to look at it.

"The eagle finally came and ate the beautiful sorghum. The older brother then cried for three days, and the eagle took pity and came to him. The older brother told the eagle the same tale of woe his younger brother had, and the eagle offered to take him to the land of gold and sun.

"When they got there, the older brother, dazzled by the great quantity of gold, could not stop gathering nuggets.

" 'Hurry, or we'll be burned to death!' the eagle cried as the sun approached.

" 'Just one more piece,' the greedy brother said.

"So the eagle flew away, and the man was burned to death."

When Tian finished, Liang, as gloomy as before, said, "What a stupid story!" Tian did not argue with him.

The sun set slowly, like a misty eye that has cried too much. Was it true that there was gold and treasure in its land? Could you really fly there on an eagle? If he ever got to that mountain of gold, how many nuggets would he take? What would he do with the money?

Liang did not ask any of those questions aloud. He did not feel like talking. Words marched in his head, but he ignored them. He waited for the night.

三十二

When the night finally came, the boys slipped back into the village and went to Tian's house.

Grandmother Liu had become talkative since her husband's death, and had picked up many of Grandfather Liu's habits, including that rumbling cough in the back of the throat. It was as though the old man had not finished his life, but had left it to his wife. Or as though she had to follow in his footsteps if she wanted to join him.

Liang could hear her even before they entered.

"What times we live in! The leader doesn't look like a leader, and the feet wander any which way. . . ."

"They're home," said Tian's mother. "Come, eat."

Liang and Tian sat down on the wide earthen bed. With Grandfather dead and Liu absent, Tian was the man of the house. He took the master's place at the center of the table, and the evening meal began. They ate in silence, except for Grandmother, who continued to chatter.

"Terrible! It's terrible! That Song girl daring to slap the prefect! . . . Tsk! . . . Those Songs aren't even from our village. At one time we were all Lius here. . . . It was the Lius who founded the Han dynasties, you know. Those were days of glory. The Liu emperors are famous for their loyalty and honesty. . . . The Lis too. You Lis founded the Tang dynasties after us. That was the most prosperous time in the whole history of our empire. That was when all the inventions were made: gunpowder, the compass, paper and printing, not to mention silk and dancing and other cultural things. Everywhere else, people were savages. Even the French, who came later and built our beautiful church. They too were barbarians in those days. . . . Then came the Song epoch, and that was when the rot set in. The Song emperors were bastards. They made no distinction between good people and bad. They were the ones who lost the Heavenly Empire to the Mongols. . . .

"So it's no surprise to me to see that girl act that way. That's the kind of family it is. Ever since her grandfather brought them here, there's been nothing but trouble.

"You know, my future prefect, since the days of our ancestors we've always buried our dead according to the principle of generations: the father ahead of the sons, each in his proper place. But the Song family doesn't do that. They bury their dead in the order of who dies first. If a son dies before his father, he gets a place in front of him. That leads to chaos. You can't tell the grandfathers from the grandsons. When people go to burn Yin banknotes at the graves of their dead on holidays, they make mistakes.

"It's terrible. . . ."

Liang cast a grateful glance at Grandmother Liu. He wanted to thank her for being so loyal, for continuing to treat him as she had before, but he felt he'd better hold his tongue. There was no point in rubbing salt in the wound.

"Grandmother," Tian said, to bring up a happier subject, "you still owe us half a story."

"What?" Grandmother Liu had trouble stopping, once she got going. She blinked in annoyance at the interruption.

"You know, the story about good and evil," Liang said.

The old woman blinked her wrinkled eyelids again. She seemed to be looking for something far in the distance.

"Oh, yes, I remember." There was a glimmer in the old woman's eyes now. "You're right. I owe you that story. That must be why I see myself telling it to you in my dreams."

With the evening meal over, the boys moved closer to the lamp to listen to Grandmother.

"Where did I leave off, the other time?" she asked.

"The poor man had just put his friend's eyes out," said Tian.

"Yes. Well, the poor man, who now was rich, put his friend's eyes out and went on to Peking alone. Since he now had a horse and a great deal of money, he reached the capital quickly. He entered the contest and won first prize. In accordance with the custom, he married the emperor's daughter and became prime minister.

"Meanwhile, the blind man, unable to reach Peking in time for the contest, became a beggar. He dared not return home, lest he cause his parents grief, so he wandered the fields, begged in the villages, and at night slept under a tree in a cemetery. In that tree were many birds, and the beggar, still determined to do good, fed them every day. The birds grew numerous, and he began to learn their language, and finally came to understand them. One day he overheard a conversation between two of them:

" 'Did you know that there's a spring at the foot of this tree?' said an owl, who could see underground.

" 'Of course,' replied a nightingale, who was the proudest bird of all. 'I know it better than you do. I also know that in the spring is a gum that can restore sight to the blind. There is also a true peony. Whoever takes that peony and gives it to the emperor can marry his favorite daughter and replace the prime minister.'

"The poor man, encouraged by this news, began to dig. He dug day and night without stopping to rest or eat, though his fingers bled. After countless days, he found the spring, the miraculous gum, and the true peony. . . ."

Grandmother Liu stopped. She had fallen asleep. A snoring sound came from her half-open mouth. The lamp flickered. The boys felt sleep creeping over them too. It was late.

"You must go to bed," Tian's mother said to them.

"I don't want to go home," Liang said to his friend.

"Then sleep here with me," said Tian.

Grandmother Liu apparently was not asleep after all, because she exclaimed, "It's a sin to spend the night elsewhere when your mother's so close by!"

"If you don't go home," added the younger woman, "the whole village will know it by tomorrow morning."

"I don't want to see my mother," Liang said.

At these words, Grandmother Liu grew very angry. She looked as though she was going to say something, but suddenly her whole body shook. Tian tapped her on the back, his mother stroked her neck, and Liang held a small bowl to her mouth for her to spit into.

The old woman finally managed to choke out a proverb: "A dog never complains of his family's poverty, nor a son of his mother's ugliness."

Accompanied by his loyal friend and protected by the night, Liang returned to his home, to his family.

三十三

"I'm home, Mama," Liang said as he crossed the threshold.

"Mama's not here."

It was his sister who said this, in a surprisingly calm, almost maternal voice. She lay under her little blanket and had raised her head slightly to speak to him.

"What do you mean?" Liang asked. "Didn't she come home?"

"Yes. She came home before noon," Ling said. "Too bad for you, Liang. You disobeyed the grownups. Mama and I had a nice lunch without you." She still didn't seem to realize what had happened that morning.

"Mama didn't look for me?"

"She did. She asked me where you went. I told her you ran off somewhere. Then she asked me what you did before . . ."

"And?"

"So I told her what you did."

His mother must have guessed that he knew what had happened to her. The pages he had read that morning had been put away. "Where is she?"

"She went to the breeding room to feed the silkworms. . . . Mama's in charge of them now. Did you know that? She's not teaching anymore."

"Why didn't you go with her?"

"I'm afraid of worms."

The breeding room, the can fang, was not far from the school. Liang turned to leave, but his sister stopped him. "Liang," she said, "please stay with me."

Liang looked at her. She seemed so tiny all alone on the big bed, curled up under her dirty blanket. She looked like a fragile silkworm herself. This was his sister. She had come into the world six years after him, was of the same flesh and blood. He remembered the things they had done together; he had never been nice to her, he had never loved her. On the night of her birth, it was raining, and after supper his mother cried out in pain. His father went for the midwife. When the midwife arrived, Liang and his father were sent out of the room. A long time later, they heard a new sound. "It's like a doll crying," Liang said.

"Not a doll," his father replied in a strange voice. "It's your sister."

For the first few days, Liang was pleased with this new presence. He and his mother ate the eggs and sweet things that the neighbors brought. He stayed home with Wang and bustled around the constantly crying baby.

"I'm going to teach my sister to read all the words I know, and I'll play with her when she grows up," he said as he and his mother sat together holding the baby. The baby's little cheeks felt like ripe persimmons.

His attitude toward Ling changed when his parents began to pay more attention to her than to him. He noticed that she always came first. Forgetting all the things he had said over her cradle, he began to hate her, and took every opportunity to avoid her company.

"Liang, don't you ever get tired of standing up all the time?" Ling asked now. "Come and sit on the bed." She knew that her brother didn't like her.

"All right." He sat on the edge of the bed. "What's all

this?" he asked, noticing that she had articles of clothing around her blanket.

"These are my friends," the little girl said, beaming. "I was playing mama and papa with them. See, this shoe looks like a boy, and those socks are babies. And I'm the mama, of course. The big boy—he's the brother—always tries to go out. He doesn't ever want to play with his sister. So I scold him. . . ."

Liang listened in silence. Without thinking, he put his hand under the blanket and rubbed her back. He was surprised at how thin her body was. He could feel the little ribs under her soft skin.

Ling looked at him with her big eyes. "You know what? Starting tomorrow, Papa's coming home for supper every night."

"Who told you that?" Liang asked sharply, jumping up.

"A man. He came here to tell us," said Ling, frightened now.

"Does Mama know?"

"No. He came after she left. But I told him I'd tell her."

"Stay here!" Liang called to his sister as he ran out the door and headed for the can fang.

Through the windows, he saw that his mother was there alone. She was leaning over tables covered with mats, distributing the leaves that the pupils had picked during the day.

"Mama," Liang tried to shout, but the shout stayed in his throat, he could not get the word out.

He realized then that something had changed. The word "Mama"—that everyday word full of all the tenderness and love a child feels for his mother—would no longer pass his lips with the old feeling. It had been taken from him. He could not say it now without feeling self-conscious. The bridge joining him to his mother had become complicated. He slipped noiselessly between the door panels and stood behind his mother.

Wang continued bending over the mats, on which thousands of silkworms swarmed. She held a bucket of water in her left hand; with her right she picked up leaves, dipped them in the water, and placed them on the mats. Now and then she would stop for a moment, but would soon have to hurry to catch up, because the worms ate quickly. She had to be careful, lest some worms eat too much and others go hungry. That would be bad for the silk.

Liang took the bucket from his mother.

"So," she said in a quiet voice, not looking at him, "I see you decided to come home. I'm glad. Did you eat at Tian's?"

"Yes," Liang answered, embarrassed.

"Good . . ." said Wang. "I know you read what I wrote this morning. You also heard what they said at the meeting, didn't you?"

Liang did not answer. He lifted the bucket a little higher so she could reach it. She dipped leaves in the water as she spoke. "I want to try to explain to you what's happened to us. Your sister is too little, and I don't want to see her life poisoned. But since you know something, you may as well know the rest."

Liang stood rigidly by his mother, a little frightened but also curious.

"Some new documents were recently discovered in the Red Army's archives. They say that your grandfather, a general under Chairman Mao, did not die in combat. They say he was not killed by the enemy at all, but was buried alive by his own comrades, on orders from above. At that time, the Chinese Communist Party was under the command of the Communist Party of the Soviet Union, which meant under the command of Stalin, its top leader. It was during the great purges in the party. . . . Well, your grandfather was accused of being a traitor, of helping the enemy."

Liang's head was spinning. He almost dropped the bucket.

"Listen, Liang," his mother said in a solemn tone, "listen carefully. One way or another, your grandfather *was* a general, maybe a revolutionary, maybe not; it's too early to tell. We are descendants of a general, and, as the old proverb says, 'A starving camel still is greater than a fat horse.' We have to stand tall.

"We will remain loyal to the Party and to Chairman Mao. And we will see what happens."

"We will see what happens!" The words echoed in Liang's head. Suddenly he felt strong again, filled by a force that seemed to come from far away, perhaps from his "traitor" grandfather. He lifted the bucket of water and nodded.

"Mama," he said, "I came to tell you that starting tomorrow, Papa will be coming home for supper."

Like a little black beetle that stops at the edge of a pit, antennae drawn back, wings folded in, Wang froze. Her hands hung over the enamel bowl in which she was kneading dough. Bits of moistened flour fell from her open palms back into the bowl.

Unable to take his eyes off his mother's hands, Liang held his breath. Only little Ling, her open mouth full of half-chewed pieces of corn bread, moved. She ran to the window. Standing on tiptoe, she raised her head to the bottom of the frame and peered out into the darkness.

It was not much of a noise they heard. It was like the slow crackling of a fire, the lazy bubbling of boiling water. Liang did not hear it so much as feel it: his whole body reacted as the sound came in from the night outside. Footsteps.

"It's Papa!" Ling shouted. She dropped her corn bread and ran to the door.

It was definitely his father's step, which was firmer and more determined than any other. If he plugged his ears, the footsteps would still echo inside him. They sounded just as they did when his father came home late from Party meetings, bringing security and sleep to the house, sleep for which Liang had waited vainly last night as he lay curled up against the wall facing the fields.

The footsteps were close now, right outside the door. In a moment it would open.

But tonight they slowed, stopped, as though gripped by hesitation at the threshold.

Ling grabbed the latch and pulled with all her might. Wang turned to watch her husband come in. Only Liang did not move. He ought to have followed his little sister's example and rushed to the door, thrown it open, and called out "Papa! Papa!" But he did not move. Something about this man approaching their door was unfamiliar to him. It was still his father, the one who had brought him up to love the Party, but now his father was no longer the district leader. The love Liang felt for his father was part of his greater love for the Party. His father had been the embodiment of the Party. But now he was a "counterrevolutionary," an "anti-Party element." It was his fault that Party directives had not been properly applied, that religion, the enemy of Communism, had not been destroyed, that revisionism was dragging the Revolution and the entire Party to ruin. How could Liang say "Papa!" with the welcome he had always felt before?

Li was standing in the doorway. He had not changed much. His eyes seemed larger, his neck a little longer, his Adam's apple more pronounced. Ling leaped into his arms. Li kissed her on the cheek and turned to Wang. "Well," he said with a smile, as though he had left the house only that morning, "what have you made for us to eat tonight?"

"The same . . . the same as always," she replied in a voice that quavered a little.

"And what about you, Liang? Aren't you helping Mama cook supper?" He put Ling down and went to help his wife.

Liang felt his stomach lurch. The unspoken word "Papa" rose to his lips again, but he could not say it. His father's brief glance did not have its former glow of strength and confidence. Instead, it showed a mixture of remorse, apology, and helplessness in the face of injustice. Liang understood that his father's look had been a plea not to judge him too harshly.

"The flames are very bright tonight," Li said, putting a cover on the iron pot in which Wang was cooking the corn bread.

Ling picked up her piece of bread and began nibbling it. There was silence except for the cricket, which sang its monotonous melancholy song in a corner of the room. Finally the silence became unbearable.

Wang looked timidly at her husband and spoke: "Is the food all right there?"

"Not too bad," Li said in a cheerful tone. "I get along well enough with the cooks. We aren't big criminals, you know, so they can't be too nasty to me."

When his wife said nothing more, he went on: "These are strange times. There's always some confusion at the beginning of a political mobilization. Mistakes are inevitable; that can't be helped. I'm the district leader, so if there are errors in the work, I have to take the responsibility."

Wang finished making the corn bread. "Even so," she said, sitting on the edge of the bed, "Song went too far. . . ."

"She dreams of power," said Li indulgently. "But she has no real sense of what's happening."

"Won't she let you come home, Papa?" asked Ling.

"Be quiet!" her mother scolded. "Children should stay out of grownup business."

"But I heard that."

"Where?"

"In the street, everywhere," said Ling with an air of triumph.

Liang could not stand much more of this. He had a

thousand questions for his father. What was going on? Who really was on the Party's side? Was his father still the district leader, the first one to receive Party directives? Why were all the things he had worked so hard for now considered anti-Party acts? Was he really a revisionist, as they said? Had he deliberately tried to sabotage the Party?

Liang wanted his father to explain it all to him. He looked up at his father's eyes. In them he saw love. But Li spoke before Liang had a chance to open his mouth: "What a well-behaved boy you've become! Have you seen Tian? Have you been helping your little sister these past few days?"

Liang began to melt. His father's voice, neither solemn nor light-hearted, struck at his heart. Something came over him that swept away politics and all the dirty little things men fought over.

"Yes, Papa!" Liang said, his voice shaking. He jumped into his father's lap.

Li held his son and stroked his hair. "Look how thin you are," he murmured. "Do you feel all right?"

Liang nodded. Huddled in his father's arms, he could see only the bottom of Li's badly shaved cheek. He thought of the rally the other day, when Song had slapped that cheek. He put out his hand to touch it, and the stubble tickled him. He felt the tickling not in his hand but in his face, because when he was little, his father had always tickled his face with a stubby cheek.

"What a good boy you are!"

The smell of sweat and bad tobacco on his father's mouth and stained fingers was sharp, raw, but also deep, like a sea Liang could float in safely. He wriggled like an ant in a burning pot, absorbing his father's smell, taking it into his blood, as though it were a force from the whole Li family.

His body, thin and tired, became a fish in tranquil water.

"Come. Supper's ready," said Wang, lifting the cover from the pot. Steam filled the room.

Then the only sounds were the smacking of lips, the chewing of teeth, and the liquid gurgles of swallowing. Liang glanced at his father, waiting for him to say something, yet also afraid that he would. His heart beat harder every time his father finished a mouthful. And Li looked at his son, secretly staring at his round, stubborn skull. Would he ever figure out what was hidden inside? Should he try to explain what had happened?

No, Li said to himself, there's no point in that.

Soon the meal would be over. Everyone now chewed slowly, as if having trouble swallowing. Only a few strips of salted vegetables remained. Then Li would have to go back.

Now they'd all stopped eating except Li. He did not look up; he pretended not to realize that the others were watching him, listening to the soft clicking of his chopsticks.

Suddenly he threw them on the table. "Enough of this!" he said.

Wang began to cry. She reached over to her husband and said: "Don't go back!"

Ling slipped between her parents and also began to cry.

It was as though a great dike had collapsed and water was flooding the land. The current too strong to be stopped with sandbags, it swept through the mountains, fields, devoured villages with a terrifying roar. Liang closed his eyes and held the water back. He did not want to cry. When grownups cried like children, children had to be grownups.

He took a step toward his father. "Papa," he said, "I'll ask them to give you permission to stay."

Liang ran out into the night before his father could

answer. He passed under the snickering poplar, brushed the corners of groaning houses, and ran like a blazing firecracker all the way to the big gate of Party headquarters.

When he got there, he stopped short, surprised that he had arrived so quickly. Under the imposing vaulted archway, he mounted the first step, feeling a black draft coming through the space between the two door panels. It blew into his face and turned the pages of memory. He had come through this gate many times. As the prefect's son, an honored guest, he had always been welcomed by the archway, respectfully greeted by the old caretaker, and by the courtyard too, which was like a wide untroubled brow.

Everything was different now. This time, he had come to ask a favor for his father, a prisoner of the Revolution.

"Who's there?" It was the caretaker's husky voice.

"It's me again."

"Oh! . . . Li Liang . . . Are you looking for your father?" babbled the old man. Liang could not see his face, but his tone seemed no different. It was still warm and kind.

"No. I've come to . . . to see . . . Comrade Song." Liang was not sure what to call her now.

"You want to see Aunt Song?" the old man said. "Wait here. I'll get her for you." He disappeared into the courtyard. But he had not let Liang in, as he used to.

Time stood still as Liang waited. He felt frightened when he realized that the Song woman would soon be standing right before him. What would he say to her? Would she bother to speak to him, a ten-year-old boy, son of an enemy of the Party? He was about to leave when he heard Song's voice in the courtyard.

"Little Liang is here? To see me? Well, let him in." Her big body came into view, with its jerky crablike walk and unpleasant smell. She walked up to Liang and stroked his hair. "You wanted to see me, little Liang? What is it?"

Liang nearly burst into tears at her warm tone. He clenched his fists and fought with all his might not to cry. It would have been better if she had been harsh, hostile.

"My father . . . he's sick."

"Sick?" said Song, surprised. "Really? He was fine a little while ago. Maybe he worked too hard in the fields this afternoon."

"I came to ask you . . . if he doesn't have to come back here tonight."

"I see." Apparently deep in thought, she paced back and forth, hands behind her back, head high, her enormous hips swaying. "So he wants to spend the night at home, does he?" she murmured, in the voice of a leader, like someone accustomed to thinking hard before deciding.

Liang blushed. Song was enjoying this.

At last she stopped pacing. "He can stay home tonight. But he must be back tomorrow morning before breakfast."

Liang said nothing. He turned and ran home.

There, all was calm. Ling lay under her blanket. Li was sitting on the bed beside her, telling her a story. Wang had cleared the table and was putting on her apron to go and feed the silkworms.

"It's taken care of!" Liang shouted joyfully. "She says it's all right!"

"Who says what's all right?" asked Li.

"Song. You can stay home tonight," said Liang, puzzled by his father's frown.

"What did you say to her?"

"I told her you were sick."

"That I was sick?" Li shouted. "You asked her, begged,

and she granted it! What gall! I'm still the leader here, even if I'm locked up, even if they kill me. If I'm locked up, it's because it's in the Party's interest, and by the decision of the Party Committee. Song has no right to make decisions of her own!"

Liang had never seen his father so angry. "But," he stammered, "I thought . . . I thought . . ."

"Calm down," his mother said. "He's too young to understand this." She turned to Liang. "Apologize to your father," she said.

"I'm sorry, Papa," Liang said, his voice faint. "I didn't realize . . ."

Li looked at his trembling son, and his anger softened. He took Liang in his arms and spoke to him seriously. "My little one, we must never act like cowards, whatever happens. If I broke down before, it was because I was with my family. But outside, we must swallow our broken teeth in silence. That's what honor means, and family. You're too young to understand it now, but when you grow up, you will."

Liang nodded, determined to understand.

"I have to go," said Wang. "The worms . . ."

"I too," said Li.

But neither of them moved. They looked at each other. Liang, watching this, wriggled out of his father's arms and said in a grown-up voice, "I'll feed the worms, Mama. You stay here with Papa for a while."

"Are you sure you can?"

"Of course. I worked with you last night."

His mother hesitated, but Liang was already out the door and heading for the can fang.

Was it a plot, a conspiracy? If it was, who was behind it? God? The Great Lord of Heaven? And who was being punished, Liang's whole family or just Liang? He remembered that he had not knelt down when the Lord of the Hearth was burned, and that he had been the one to scale the steeple to destroy the ten at the top of it. Was God now taking revenge?

He lay rigid in the nest of his blanket, racked by fear and remorse. He had been lying absolutely motionless for an hour, reliving the scene that took place just before dawn, when his mother came back from giving the silkworms their last night feeding.

"Liang, wake up!" she had said. "Liang, this is terrible! Did you forget to wash the leaves?. . . They're covered with sulfates, and most of the worms are dead!"

Liang heard the panic in his mother's voice. He rubbed his eyes and said, "I can't remember if I did or not. . . ."

This was not true. He remembered very well. His mind had been elsewhere when he went to the can fang alone after supper. His father's words were still echoing in his head. He had definitely forgotten to wash the leaves. In fact, he remembered wondering why the job took less time than the night before. He had taken a shortcut, and because of that his mother, too, was now locked up, accused of trying to destroy the Revolution by killing the silkworms.

三十五

The melon guard, vice-chairman of the revolutionary committee, had sent two men to take her away. It felt as though a hundred years had passed since then. Ling lay asleep beside him, not knowing that her mother would not be there when she woke up. And it was all Liang's fault. He had been so upset, he pretended he couldn't remember, and his mother had had to take the blame for feeding the worms leaves covered with sulfate. He should have been braver, honest; he should have told his mother, yes, he had forgotten to wash the leaves. When the men came to take her away, he should have jumped up and screamed at the top of his lungs, "Lock me up, not my mother!" Instead, he had stayed in bed without saying a word. But maybe that was because he had been half-asleep and couldn't think straight. He wasn't sure. It had been an exhausting day.

The first bird calls could be heard. Ling's small body turned over. That was the third time. On the fourth, she would wake up. And when she did, she would call, "Mama! Mama!" That was always her way of starting a new day. She did it even when she knew her mother was not there. What could he answer? "Mama's not here, she went to work." That was what he usually said. But today? "Mama has been locked up . . . because of me."

If you can hate yourself, you ought to be able to punish yourself too; that way you can do justice and also stop the pain boring into your heart.

"Liang!" his little sister called, turning over.

"What?" Liang answered, looking at her.

She smiled, her eyes open wide, her hair disheveled.

"Are you awake?" Liang asked. He stared at her suspiciously. Why had she called for him instead of for Mama? Did she know what had happened? Had she only been pretending to be asleep?

"I think I had a dream last night, Liang," she said plaintively.

Liang sat up. "Do you want me to help you dress?"

"No," she said. "I've known how to get dressed by myself for a long time. I just never did it when there were grownups around."

Liang began to put on his clothes, watching Ling all the while. She still had not asked for her mother. He decided to say nothing and began to prepare breakfast.

Imitating his mother, he put some rice in the pot, washed it, and placed it on the stove, which was always lit. Soon the water began to bubble. He took a piece of salted vegetable out of the big jar on the floor, washed it, and began to cut it into strips.

Ling finished dressing, got out of bed barefoot, and stood at the mirror to comb her hair. The way she held the comb and pushed back the locks of hair made her look very grown up.

But when he put the food on the low table, she sat sulking in the corner behind the door. She refused to eat.

"I want Mama."

"Mama . . . will be home soon. We have to eat first."

"I want Mama." Ling wasn't interested in her brother's explanation. "I want Mama."

"I just told you. She can't eat with us. If you don't eat, I'll eat it all, and I won't leave any for you."

"I want Mama."

Ling repeated the words in a sullen, monotonous voice, like the buzzing of a big green fly.

The buzzing gripped Liang's heart. It made his head spin.

"I want Mama."

"You want Mama, you want Mama! But you can't have

her!" he screamed. He jumped over to his sister and pushed her hard. "It's my fault!" he shouted. "It's all because of me!"

He opened the door and ran off.

"No!" the melon guard snapped. "Absolutely out of the question." He was sitting behind a desk, with several people wearing red armbands around him. Aunt Song was not among them.

Liang tried again. "But I told you, it was my fault."

"Out of the question. If it really was your fault, that's all the more reason to lock her up. We gave her this task because we had confidence in her. If she turned such an important assignment over to a ten-year-old child instead of working hard to reeducate herself, then that is proof of her backwardness."

"But I'm the guilty one," Liang persisted.

"The answer is no. Now get out of here! Go on, get out!"

The melon guard got up, took Liang by the arm, and dragged him out.

But once they were outside the office, his attitude changed completely. "Listen," he whispered, almost kindly, "you better get going, or they'll lock you up too. Do you know how much we paid for those silkworms? More than two hundred yuan! What could we say to the Party if we didn't lock your mother up? I know it's hard for you and your sister—she's four, isn't she?—but we won't keep your mother long, just a few days, until all this blows over."

He walked with Liang as far as the gate. "Go on home," he said, and added, with a wink, "If you can't cook for yourself, why don't you come over to my house with your sister? My wife is always home."

As Liang watched him walk back to the office, he thought that the man must have married a very beautiful woman after the rich harvest in Xin Zhuang.

三十六

The moon slipped silently from behind the clouds, and the little window frame seemed to move with it. It was almost a full moon, so it must have been the thirteenth or fourteenth day of the lunar month. "If the moon is not round on the fifteenth, it will be round on the sixteenth," the proverb said.

Liang could see the moon clearly from his part of the bed. He had never looked at it so carefully before. The first time he had really noticed the moon was one night in the town. He was with old Huang, the caretaker of the Party Committee office, who was almost, but not quite, blind. "You people talk about stars all the time," Huang said, "but I'll believe it when I see them with my own eyes and not before."

"Look up at the sky, Grandfather Huang," Liang said that night, in an effort to convince him. "All those shiny things are stars."

The old man took Liang's hand apologetically. "Little Liang," he said, "you're such a nice boy, and I know I ought to believe you, because children never lie. But this one time I just can't go along with you. Grownups make fun of me, they say I'll believe anything."

"But Grandfather . . ."

"No, Liang. You may as well forget it."

Liang looked sadly at the stars. Suddenly he had an idea. "What about that?" he asked, pointing at the moon. "Do you believe that, at least?"

Old Huang slowly raised his head, which looked like a strangely shaped melon, and blinked his eyes, which were two little nests of wrinkles.

"There!" Liang said, taking the old man's finger and pointing it in the direction of the moon. Luckily, the moon was very bright that night. The old man nodded.

"Yes. I can see that," he said. "Yes. Something very pale."

"Well, that's the moon!" Liang exclaimed, triumphant.

But there wasn't much you could do if a person really didn't want to believe something.

He almost laughed now, but he stopped himself. He did not want to wake his little sister. It hadn't been easy to get her to go to sleep. He watched the lovely moon in silence, and the slowly moving clouds. There were so many of them. It was as if they ducked into some secret passageway after they went by, then came out again and again. Perhaps they were trying to blot out the moon. But the moon always won. It had such a wonderful light, not dazzling like the arrogant sun, but sweet and pleasant. If you looked at it, it looked back at you. If you said something to it, it seemed to understand. If your heart was heavy, as Liang's was tonight, you could look at it and it would lift the weight and make you feel happy again. Not happy, maybe, but sort of comfortably sad. And if you had tears in your eyes, it looked even more beautiful: little stars glittered on its body to cheer you up, to remove the sobs rising in your throat.

Does the moon know everything that happens on the earth below? Liang almost asked the question out loud, but he already knew the answer: Of course it did.

"Heaven knows everything," Grandfather Liu always used to say. By now he might be a child in a revolutionary family. Grandfather Liu had told Liang that a man has another life after he dies. If he's been good, he'll be reborn into a noble family and suffer no more grief. But if he's been bad, he'll become a dog, or, worse, a pig to be slaughtered.

"You must have been an ape, you're so mischievous," Grandmother Liu used to say whenever Tian played some trick. At that time, Liang had thought that the man he had been before must have been very good, because Liang had been born into this life as the son of a prefect and the grandson of a general. Now, he didn't want to think about that, not with his mother and father both locked up. He was alone with his little sister. What sin had his former self committed, for him to suffer such misfortune? And what could he do to make sure he would not have this kind of misfortune in his next life?

Suddenly he heard tapping on the window. He jumped and called out, "Who's there?"

"It's me." The voice of an old woman.

"Who?"

"Grandmother Song." Her voice seemed choked with sobs.

"What do you want?"

"I . . . I want to talk to you."

Liang hesitated, but finally opened the window and looked out. Grandmother Song was leaning against the wall, holding a white package.

Liang did not know what to say.

The old woman looked at him. "Hurry, let me in," she said. "I brought you some pancakes. The little one likes them." She held up the package and gestured.

Liang went out to open the gate and waited for the old woman to walk around to the front of the school to get in.

She headed straight for their room without a word, her white package swinging like a third hand. She lit the lamp, put the package on the table, and sat down on the edge of the bed near Ling's head. As she leaned over the little girl, her eyes were wet with tears.

"Has she been asleep long?" Grandmother Song asked in a hushed voice.

"Yes."

"Did she eat anything before she went to bed?" She softly brushed back a lock of the little girl's hair.

"Yes."

The old woman had cut her hair short, like all the women now in the district. She leaned closer to Ling, as though she were going to kiss her, then dabbed at her own eyes with the dirty hem of her jacket.

"Oh, my little one, my little one," she crooned, "it's been so long since you've come to see me. You left your dear grandmother all alone. I think about you all the time, I cry for you every day."

Liang stood behind her as she sobbed quietly. He was not sure whether to comfort the old woman or ask her to leave. After all, it was because of her daughter that all this had happened. Then he realized that he was crying too, so he decided to let her stay.

"Do you want me to wake her up?" he asked.

"No, don't do that. Don't disturb her. It makes me feel better just to look at her." She got up, walked around the room three times, then shuffled to the door, her steps as tiny as her feet, which looked like two dumplings.

Then she turned and spoke to Liang in an imploring tone: "Dear little boy, please bring her, at nightfall tomorrow, to the road leading out of the village. I want to take her to my sister's house for a few days."

Liang did not answer.

"It's in another village. No one will know, I promise. I swear it in the name of the Lord of Heaven . . . I mean, in the name of Chairman Mao. . . ."

She looked at Liang again with pleading eyes. He finally nodded.

Grandmother hoisted Ling onto her scrawny back and set out unsteadily on the dusty road that led to a neighboring village.

Liang felt both relieved and uneasy. He watched them for a while before turning toward home. He had to cross the main street, which he hadn't seen since the great rally.

It was almost deserted in the dusk. The walls were covered with dazibaos torn by the wind but still readable. They were mostly denunciations, and many contained accusations against his father and mother, whose names were crossed out in red. Liang did not understand a lot of what was written, but he saw a few drawings that were quite clear. One large poster depicted his father as a wolf carrying his mother, drawn as a weasel, on his back. "The alliance of the wolf and the weasel," read the caption. Liang remembered the story about the two animals; his mother had told it to him during a happy evening at home.

"The wolf is wicked and strong, but he has no ideas. The weasel is very crafty, but she can go nowhere, because her front paws are too short. So they make an alliance. The wolf will carry the weasel on his back so she can travel faster, and the weasel will whisper wicked ideas to the wolf. Together they go around doing mischief."

Liang was surprised to see himself in the drawing. He was depicted as a black fang that

protruded from the wolf's mouth and shouted: "I want to bite the fruits of the Revolution."

"Don't move!" His whole body shuddered when he heard the voice behind him. It sounded military, like the Red Army in a war movie sneaking up on the enemy. A command in that tone, and the enemy surrenders. It had become a game among the village children, so Liang thought someone must be playing it now. He turned around slowly, raising his arms over his head the way enemy soldiers did in the movies.

"This is not a joke," said the voice.

Liang saw a tall boy with a pale face. He must have been more than seventeen, because Liang had never seen him in school. "What's wrong?" he asked.

"You were reading those dazibaos, weren't you?" the boy said, making sure Liang saw the Red Guard band on his left arm.

Liang did not know what to say.

"Answer me!"

"Yes."

"Good. You read that one for me." The boy pointed to a poster with large characters that said, "Down with Li Xian Yang, traitor to the Revolution!"

Liang looked at the poster. The characters suddenly seemed to be a challenge.

"Read it. If you don't, it's proof you're a counterrevolutionary," the boy said, grabbing Liang by the ear. "Read that poster out loud!"

Liang felt a fire in his ear. Hatred closed his throat as a padlock locks a wooden trunk.

"Read it to me!" the boy snarled, pinching Liang's ear harder.

Liang heard his enemy's knuckles crack. He turned his head and stared into the boy's eyes.

"No!"

Liang's pain vanished when he barked out that answer. A force from within him had filled his voice, his "No!" He closed his eyes, feeling calm. It was as though a vase brimming with fear and hatred had been hanging from a rope over an abyss, and his answer had cut the rope. All he had to do was let the vase fall and break. His anguish and anxiety were gone.

The boy stopped twisting his ear, but shouted again: "Read it to me!"

When Liang still stood silent, the boy finally let go of his ear. They looked at each other. Full night had fallen, and dogs were barking somewhere.

"You're all right," the boy said, punching Liang lightly in the shoulder. "You're not a coward."

In the dark Liang found it hard to read the expression in his enemy's eyes.

"Where are you going?" the boy asked, now friendly.

"I don't know . . ." Liang replied quietly. "Home, I guess."

"But there's no one there. It must be lonely."

Liang felt a sob catch in his throat. He swallowed hard to force it down.

"Why don't you come to our house? Uncle Old Black will tell you lots of good stories."

"Uncle Old Black!" A shudder went through Liang like an electric shock at the mention of the name.

"Yes. Uncle Old Black. I spend a lot of evenings with him, sometimes all night. He has a big warm bed. Come on. You don't seem as bad as it says on the dazibaos."

The boy took Liang by the arm, and Liang let himself be pulled along. He remembered Grandfather Liu saying, "Old Black is the only one who's ever seen it," when they had spoken about the Wen Meng.

They walked side by side in the darkness. Liang felt that this new, unexpected friend was leading him into a doubtful adventure. The name Uncle Old Black had come up more than once, about strange things. Mass was held in his house; he was the one who gave permission for funerals to start; he was the only man who was said to have seen the mysterious animal that uttered that terrible cry. Liang was both scared and curious, as if on a road that would lead him to another world. He had seen Uncle Old Black once before, at the mass: an old man with a black beard and white clothes, but he remembered no particular feature of his face.

"So today's the day I'll finally meet him," Liang said, not quite out loud.

"What did you say?" the tall boy asked.

"Nothing."

"You've never seen Uncle Old Black?"

"No." Liang was not sure whether he was lying or telling the truth.

"I'm sure he knows you."

They came to a closed door. Liang let his companion enter first.

"Uncle!" the boy called out as he crossed the threshold.

"Well, well," a very old voice said in reply.

The tall boy walked straight through the courtyard, with Liang following.

There was no light in the old man's room. It was completely black.

"Uncle," the tall boy said in the darkness, "I've brought a kid to see you: the prefect's son."

Liang stopped on the steps leading to the door, waiting for a light.

"Come on in, my future prefect," the old man drawled.

Liang dared wait no longer. He went in, his scalp crawling. A red spark winked in the darkness, lighting a patch of earthen wall.

"Can't we light a lamp?" Liang asked timidly.

"If you want," the old man replied indifferently.

"I'll get some matches," said the tall boy, and he began to rummage in the dark. He made a lot of noise as he lifted the mat under the bed and searched around the room. The red spark blinked a little more strongly, as though to assert its presence before the lamp was lit. Was this the old man's pipe? Or was it something else . . . ?

Finally a tiny oil lamp was lit, but it was barely able to dispel the dark. Liang was relieved to see that the red light indeed came from a pipe. He sat down on the bed very slowly, not daring to rest his full weight on the edge.

"You sit on the bed very nicely," the old man said.

Liang almost fell off. Uncle Old Black was blind.

"Your name is Liang, isn't it?"

Liang was unable to say a word, so the tall boy answered for him: "Yes, that's Li Liang. But he's a good kid, not like it says on the dazibaos."

"Well, it could hardly be otherwise, if he's the true son of a prefect," the blind man murmured, drawing on his pipe, which whistled with each puff. "But I knew that the first time he came here."

Liang now remembered that the night he and Tian had been there, the old man had turned his head in their direction. But wasn't the old man blind?

"Good people are always forced to suffer trials," Uncle Old Black said. "And the trials are harsh indeed. Look at what Jesus Christ suffered before he was nailed to the cross and became God. The great General Han Xin, who helped Emperor Liu found his dynasty, fell under the heel of a filthy bastard. Confucius, in his time, was driven out of many a kingdom and suffered many insults. Sun Zi, China's greatest strategist, was able to write his famous books because he was locked up and had his knees shattered. The famous poet Li Bai was angry at nearly everyone throughout his life. Emperor Li had a terrible childhood. . . . Our ancestors put it exactly right: 'To make a man great on this earth, heaven first fills his heart with bitterness, hardens his body with weariness, and tempers his will with unhappiness.' "

The old man rambled on, his mouth hidden by his pipe and beard. He seemed to take boundless pleasure in talking. Liang understood little of what he said, though he knew the famous names. His fear was gone. He stopped listening to this old man, and thought about the one question he had: Have you seen the Wen Meng?

But Uncle Old Black was blind. Why, then, did everyone say that he was the only one who had seen the animal? Had he gone blind only after seeing it? Had the animal somehow caused him to lose his sight? Or was he able to see it precisely because he was blind?

"It's getting late," said the tall boy, bored with the old man's chatter. "I have to go home."

He left. Liang stayed. The lamp grew dim, and the dark began to reclaim the room.

"Uncle Old Black," Liang said in a strange voice, "there's something I wanted to ask you."

"Something you wanted to ask me?" The old man broke

off his monologue and blinked in bewilderment. "A question, a question . . ."

"Yes, a question." Liang tried to stop himself, but could not: "Is it true that you have seen—"

"No! Stop!" the old man shouted. "My death, you mean?"

Liang was struck dumb. He sat still, unable to move.

"Time to go to bed," the old man said in a voice that sounded almost malicious. He stretched out along the wall.

Liang did not move. He sat on the edge of the bed and waited. The little lamp flickered one last time and went out. Liang sank into a black well of questions. Why had the old man acted so strangely? Why had Liang been stopped from asking his question? Had Grandfather Liu's death been caused by that same question? How could there be any connection between a question and a human life? Liang seemed to be the only one in the world trying to find out more. Was he also the only one who had heard the sound?

Uncle Old Black began to snore, and the snoring made Liang sleepy. He stretched out on the wide bed.

The round moon was slowly climbing higher in the window frame. Liang had never spent the night under a window so big that it felt as though he were sleeping in the open air, directly under the moon. He closed his eyes, looked at the inside of his eyelids, and saw preposterous images.

Among the images was a big red star, the old man's pipe. Liang was not surprised. He watched the old man as he smoked, making sparks.

When had the old man begun to speak again? Liang had no idea. He just listened.

"Oh, yes, my little Liang, I won't hide it from you anymore. . . . I do know the secret of that sound. It's not an animal's cry. It's not a cry at all, but a song, the song of the earth's soul. You're lucky to have heard it, for it is not often that the earth sings, and not everyone can hear it. The earth sings when it is happy, and only a man who has a soul can hear it.

"It's a song, the song of the earth's soul."

Liang listened, peaceful, happy. His sorrows were forgotten. They could no longer reach him. He soared high in the sky.

The moon moved on, pulling dawn after it, up from the horizon.

三十九

That same yellow earth now had shiny white crusts. The sorghum plants looked like sickly spiders as they leaned their fragile heads together in groups and tried to escape the salt's attack. Collapsed wells made darker patches among the wild vegetation that struggled in the dust. The wind blew. The few trees, isolated and abandoned in the fields, sang a melancholy song.

The sun sank behind the western hills, fleeing a pack of black and crimson clouds. A crow with gleaming feathers, fat with prey, gave a menacing shriek.

The ribbon of road, broad here, narrow there, snaked dark ocher through the yellow of the fields, fields stretching out between arms of the earth, who was indifferent to the violence done to its ravaged soil.

The old cart carrying the family's things was all that moved in this motionless world. It rolled slowly toward the darkening east, toward its destiny, with a creak like a distant laugh.

Where was that barely noticeable smell coming from? It seemed to be carried by the night. Liang sniffed, moving his head from side to side like a cat. It was neither the sugary odor of the sorghum nor the bitter dust the wind now and then lifted off the salt crusts. It was more like the smell of the setting sun, a smell that rose out of the depths of the earth at the approach of summer, heralding drought. A worse drought this time.

Liang walked slightly behind his father. He had decided this was the best position. He bent forward and pulled as hard as he could on the rope looped over his shoulder. He had to lean hard to get the wheels over a small ridge in the road, but the rope bit deeper into his shoulder. His father skidded in the dust, dragged back by the weight. They inched along, fighting for ground. Sometimes Liang thought the road was an enormous wheel that turned in the direction opposite to their progress, so that no matter how they moved, they stayed in the same place.

Li pulled the cart along without a word, his panting merged with the rhythm of his steps and the creaking of the axle. Liang felt guilty about his father's silence. Maybe he should not have contradicted him earlier. After Li had loaded the cart, he had turned to Liang and his sister and said, "Get in. It's time to go." He had spoken the words with a smile and with that same good-natured air he'd had when he told them they were leaving—not to go back to the town, but to move on to Liang's grandfather's village, the place where he'd spent the spring holiday.

"No," Liang had said stubbornly as his sister climbed into the cart, clutching her doll.

"What's the matter?" Li asked.

"I'll help you pull the cart."

Liang's father was embarrassed. "It's not heavy. You'll only slow us down."

But Wang, putting her hand on her son's head, asked him, "Do you think you're strong enough?"

Liang looked his father in the eye, clenched his teeth, and nodded.

"Maybe it'll help a little," Wang said to Li.

Li rummaged in the old sack that hung from the shaft of the cart and took out a dirty rope. With suddenly trembling fingers, he tied a slipknot, which Liang draped over his shoulder. The other end was tied to the cart.

His father had not spoken since then. If he had climbed into the cart like his sister and let himself be pulled along, maybe Li would still be in a good mood. Maybe he would have continued telling stories. "Pull a cart? That's nothing! Who needs a donkey? This way you don't have to worry about what the donkey's going to do. And we know that once a donkey has his mind set on something, that's it. I pulled plenty of carts when I was in the Red Army . . . even a cannon, along with two comrades. And under enemy fire!"

But now he was sad, silent. He knew that Liang understood, that Liang had not been fooled by his father's lies. They had been driven out of the village. How terrible it must be for a father to know that his son thinks of him as an enemy of the Party, the Party he has brought him up to love so much!

Liang wished he didn't understand. If only he could be as innocent as he was before! Things had been so much simpler when he knew nothing and believed whatever the grownups said. Then he could have thought that they were just going to live with their uncles and cousins, where they would feel at home. That, even if they were going to be peasants, they could still be happy.

But no! He had to face the truth. Revisionists! A traitor's daughter! The whole family disgraced, expelled. They were not allowed to have jobs. They were no longer Party cadres, only peasants who had to return to their native village to feed themselves by tilling the soil. Liang was miserable, and he knew that this added to his father's misery. A vicious circle of misery.

Liang walked as fast as he could to take up the slack in the rope. Ling had been jostled awake by the bumps in the road, and now sat in the driver's seat, urging on her father as he had once urged on the donkey. She was delighted with her perch in that grown-up place. Wang, carrying a bag, brought up the rear. She walked along silently, a shadow of their shadow, a shadow of herself.

And their shadows lengthened in the twilight. The last glimmers of day streaked the darkening sky with violets and blues.

The road curved around a hill. Two silhouettes suddenly appeared under a tree, one tall and bulky, the other small and frail: Liu and his son, Tian.

Liang tried to look nonchalant. He wanted it to be clear that his father was pulling the cart all by himself.

When they reached the tree, they stopped. They all looked at one another in silence. Liu's lips moved, but no sound came out. He seemed embarrassed, like a child who has broken his rice bowl.

"Prefect Li," he finally said. "You're leaving. . . . I wish you a good journey."

Li tried to smile. "Well, it's not very far," he said, gesturing down the road.

The two men fell silent. They gazed off into the fields.

Tian ran over to Liang. "I don't want you to go!" he said loudly.

Liang hugged him. "I'll come and see you. Two years from now, I'll be able to get a bicycle. Then I'll come, and we can go for walks again with the white goat, and . . ."

He could not finish. There was a lump in his throat, and his eyes filled with tears. Crying, the two boys embraced.

Wang kissed them both and said, "Now, you're growing up. You don't want to cry like babies. The villages aren't so far apart, after all. You'll see each other again."

Tian and Liang were ashamed. They tried to smile like men.

"I'll come and see you next Sunday," said Tian, chewing on a finger. "I have an aunt who lives near your village."

"I'll be waiting for you," Liang said through his clenched teeth.

"The sorghum seems to be doing pretty well in this field," Li said in the important voice he had used when he was still a prefect. Liang was probably the only one who heard the sadness in it.

"Yes. Thanks to all the work we did last year," Liu replied, without enthusiasm. "But soon it'll all be scorched by drought."

Li looked at the wells they had dug. Nearly all of them had collapsed. Suddenly his cheeks were sucked in and his lips trembled. Liang watched as his father's face became a mask like the one worn by the villain in the third act so the audience will know when to boo and jeer. All these months, Liang thought, the play had been building to this image of his father.

And in his own body he felt his father's pain.

Li pulled himself together, swallowed, and said, "You know, Liu, I am convinced that the Communist Party was right to launch this movement. The class struggle has to be our prime objective. Chairman Mao's revolutionary line must not be compromised by the needs of production. Think about it. If we had continued as we began, we would have brought in better and better harvests, more and more grain. We would have become rich, we would have become bourgeois. We made the Revolution with Mao to overthrow the bourgeoisie, so what would have become of the Revolution had we turned into the bourgeoisie ourselves?"

Li stopped, apparently surprised by what he had just said. He smiled at Liu and added, under his breath, "We can always learn from the Party."

"Yes . . . I guess so," Liu stammered, pulling Tian close to him to clear a path for the cart.

Li picked up the poles, and Liang took the rope. The cart began to move again as Wang said a few words about Tian's studies and asked Liu to give her regards to his wife.

"Prefect Li, there's no need for you to . . ."

Liu's phrase was lost in the creaking of the cart, and Liang barely had time to glimpse his friend's smile. The road carried them away from one another.

The sun had gone down, the wind had died, but there was still a hazy light near the ground. Liang could see his father's back in front of him. His spine showed through his sweat-stained shirt.

After another bend in the road, the cart passed the field where the graves of the Liu family were. They lay under an acacia with twisted branches and were covered with grass that made them look like broad-brimmed hats of bristly, worn-out straw. Young shoots were sprouting among the yellow grass that had died the winter before. As though afraid of the long oncoming night, the poor graves tried to draw closer together. You could almost hear the unhappy dead, silent, tender, moving ever closer under the grass, yet unable to meet.

Liang looked for Grandfather Liu's grave. It was by itself, away from the others. His brothers and sisters were still alive, so he had no companions. What did he have to look forward to as night fell? A few people on the road, a familiar creaking cart, belated greetings from the living? Yes, Grandfather Liu, Liang says hello.

Liang remembered what the old man looked like when they pulled him from the wreckage of the kiln, his mouth wide open and his face ruined, but he also remembered how he looked sitting happily behind his potter's wheel, turning mud into clay bowls.

When Grandfather Liu got up from the table after a good meal, he would sit in the warmest spot on the edge of the bed and smoke his long-stemmed wooden pipe under the halo of light from the oil lamp. "Food is the god of the people," he would murmur. He had died trying to save his kiln and his bowls. Then the Cultural Revolution came, and the kiln, repaired after his death, was abandoned. His bowls lay unused. What good were they when there was no grain?

The cart rolled on, leaving the cemetery behind. They passed a broad field of corn, taller than the sorghum but thinner and more sparse. This field too was dotted by the great dark wounds of collapsed wells. Li slowed down and stared into the immense field in which he had toiled day and night. In the distance was the irrigation ditch for which he had nearly paid with his life. Liang slowed down too. There was a kind of pleasure in the fatigue that swept over his neck, his back, his legs. It was as if he could hold his suffering in check or let it go, as if he had some unknown energy, some magical power that could relieve his father's pain, a current that could pass from his body to his father's, a dark secret river, sometimes sluggish, sometimes lively and strong, and if normally the river flowed downstream, from the mountains to the sea, today its course had been reversed, today Liang was giving life to his father.

In front of him walked a weary man whose face he could not see, except for the flash of profile when his father turned to look at the corn. Liang felt the stiffness of his father's neck, the clench of his father's jaws. Through the cart's poles he felt the trembling of his father's limbs.

After a few more steps, Li stopped. Liang, in a burst of understanding, summoned all his strength and grabbed a pole to prevent the cart from tipping backward.

His father turned his head and glanced gratefully at Liang. Then he turned back, with a sharp gesture Liang had never seen him make before, and set out again.

The cart moved on. Li took such long strides, Liang had to trot to keep up with him. Ling yelled that she couldn't stand the jolts. Wang, silent and alone, seemed lost in thought.

Li walked on, paying no attention. Confusing questions swirled through Liang's head as he ran like a young ox in harness for the first time.

The cart moved on into the night. . . .